DANCE HALL OF THE DEAD

THE EXCHANGE

Should some
mysteries be
left unsolved?

DANCE HALL OF THE DEAD

TONY HILLERMAN

 HAMPTON-BROWN

Dance Hall of the Dead by Tony Hillerman, Copyright © 1973 by Anthony G. Hillerman.
Cover art by Peter Thorpe. This edition is published by arrangement with HarperCollins Publishers.
All rights reserved.

Cover photograph of desert © by Digital Stock.
Illustration on p.11 © by Peter Thorpe.

On-Page Coach™ (introductions, questions, on-page glossaries), The Exchange,
back cover summary © Hampton-Brown.

Hampton-Brown
P.O. Box 223220
Carmel, California 93922
800-333-3510
www.hampton-brown.com

Printed in the United States of America

ISBN 13: 978-0-7362-3168-8
ISBN 10: 0-7362-3168-4

06 07 08 09 10 11 12 13 14 15 10 9 8 7 6 5 4 3 2 1

For Alex Atcitty and Old Man Madman and all the others who agree that Custer had it coming

Author's Note

In this book, the setting is genuine. The Village of Zuñi and the landscape of the Zuñi reservation and the adjoining Ramah Navajo reservation are accurately depicted to the best of my ability. The characters are purely fictional. The view the reader receives of the Shalako religion is as it might be seen by a Navajo with an interest in ethnology. It does not pretend to be more than that.

Introduction

Dance Hall of the Dead is a modern detective story that focuses on **native** Indian **cultures** in the American Southwest. It tells a story about the disappearance of two teenage boys. One is Zuñi. The other is Navajo. The events in the story take place on the Zuñi and Navajo reservations where the missing teenagers lived.

Until the mid-nineteenth century, Native American tribes in the West fought to save their land from U.S. settlers. After decades of fighting, Native Americans lost most of their land. Settlers built their farms, ranches, and towns. And the United States government forced the native tribes onto the remaining small areas of land called reservations. Native Americans had no choice but to move there.

Over 300 Indian reservations exist in the United States. Each is managed by a Native American tribe. The tribes work to preserve their native languages and practice their tribal **customs**. Reservations have their own laws and system of government, called the tribal council. The Zuñi and Navajo reservations are located near each other in the southwestern

Key Concepts

native *adj.* from or of a particular area
culture *n.* beliefs, practices, and customs
custom *n.* traditional habit of one particular group

United States, but they have separate police forces, laws, and government.

The Navajo and Zuñi also have very different **spiritual** beliefs. *Dance Hall of the Dead* focuses on the secretive religion of the Zuñi tribe. The story begins days before the Shalako ceremony. The Shalako are the ancestor spirits who communicate between the gods and the Zuñi people. They deliver blessings and carry messages, such as prayers for rain. The ceremony to honor them is a sacred event. The Shalako are welcomed and honored with feasting and dancing.

A few special Zuñi men are chosen to dance in the Shalako ceremony. Each man wears a mask to represent a different Shalako spirit. To dance in the ceremony is considered a great honor. But the dancing is very hard. The men practice for the ceremony all year.

There are some parts of the Zuñi religion that only its members know. The Zuñi are very private about their beliefs. They are so protective of their practices that it is **taboo** to reveal certain details of their religion to outsiders.

Dance Hall of the Dead is a detective novel filled with twists and turns. This type of mystery story centers on a crime, which is usually a murder. The reader follows the main character as he or she tries to find the killer. Each new clue leads to a plot twist that keeps the reader guessing about who really committed the crime.

Tony Hillerman is famous for writing mysteries. He is the former president of the Mystery Writers of America. He has written more than a dozen mysteries about Native American

Key Concepts

spiritual *adj.* of or relating to religion

taboo *adj.* forbidden

The Zuñi and the Navajo

- Although the Zuñi and Navajo reservations are near one another, the cultures of these tribes are different.

- The Zuñi people's ancestry can be traced back to the Anasazi people. The Anasazi (meaning "Ancient Ones") existed over two thousand years ago. Religion was very important to the Anasazis. It was connected to all their activities.

- The Navajo people's ancestry can be traced back to the Athabascan people. The Athabascan came from Asia about 35,000 years ago. The Navajo divided from this group about 1,000 years ago.

- A basic cultural difference between the Anasazi and the Athbascan is that the Anasazis were concerned with the group as a whole, without much regard for the individual. The Athabascan considered the individual more important.

cultures. Hillerman has won the Special Friends of the Dinee Award from the Navajo Nation. The Navajos gave the award to Hillerman for his accurate description of the Navajo. Hillerman's talent for writing and his knowledge of Native American culture gives readers a fascinating look into the beliefs and customs of Native Americans.

1

Sunday, November 30, 5:18 P.M.

Shulawitsi, the Little Fire God, member of the Council of the Gods and Deputy to the Sun, had taped his track shoes to his feet. He had wound the tape as Coach taught him, tight over the arch of the foot. And now the spikes biting into the packed earth of the sheep trail seemed a part of him. He ran with perfectly conditioned grace, his body a machine in motion, his mind detached, attending other things. Just ahead where the trail shifted down the slope of the **mesa** he would stop—as he always did—and check his time and allow himself four minutes of rest. He knew now with an exultant certainty that he would be ready. His lungs had expanded, his leg muscles hardened. In two days when he led Longhorn and the Council from the ancestral village to Zuñi, **fatigue** would not cause him to forget the words of the great chant, or make any missteps in the ritual dance. And when **Shalako** came he would be ready to dance all the night without an error. The **Salamobia** would never have to punish him. He remembered the year when he was nine, and Hu-tu-tu had stumbled on the causeway over Zuñi Wash, and the Salamobia had struck him with their yucca wands and

....

mesa small, flat area in the mountains
fatigue tiredness; exhaustion
Shalako the Zuñi religious ceremony
Salamobia Zuñi warrior spirit that punishes people

everyone had laughed. Even the Navajos had laughed, and they laughed very little at Shalako. They would not laugh at him.

The Fire God half fell onto the outcropping of rock that was his regular resting place. He glanced quickly at his watch. He had used eleven minutes and fourteen seconds on this lap—cutting eleven seconds off his time of yesterday. The thought gave him satisfaction, but it faded quickly. He sat on the outcrop, a slender boy with black hair falling damp across his forehead, massaging his legs through the cotton of his sweat pants. The memory of the laughing Navajos had turned his thoughts to George Bowlegs. He approached these thoughts gingerly, careful to avoid any anger. It was always to be avoided, but now it was strictly taboo. The **Koyemshi** had appeared in the village two days ago, announcing in each of the four plazas of Zuñi that eight days hence the **Shalako** would come from the Dance Hall of the Dead to visit their people and bless them. This was no time for angry thoughts. Bowlegs was his friend, but Bowlegs was crazy. And he had reason to be angry with him if the season did not forbid it. George had asked too many questions, and since George was a friend he had given more answers than he should have given. No matter how badly he wanted to be a Zuñi, to join the Fire God's own Badger Clan, George was still a Navajo. He had not been **initiated**, had not felt the darkness of the mask slip over his head, and seen through the eyes of the kachina spirit. And therefore there were things that George was not allowed to know and some of those things, the Fire God thought glumly, he might have told

....

Koyemshi sacred clown

Shalako ancestral spirits and messengers of the gods

initiated allowed to join the Zuñi tribe by going through the necessary rituals

George. Father Ingles didn't think so, but Father Ingles was a white man.

Behind him, above the red sandstone wall of the mesa, a skyscape of feathery cirrus clouds stretched southward toward Mexico. To the west over the Painted Desert, they were flushed with the afterglow of sunset. To the north this reflected light colored the cliffs of the Zuñi Buttes a delicate rose. Far below him in the shadow of the mesa, a light went on in the camper near the **site of the anthropologist's dig**. Ted Isaacs cooking supper, the Fire God thought. And that was another thing not to think about, to avoid being angry with George. It had been George's idea to see if they could find some of the things made by the Old People in the Doctor's box of chips and beads and arrowheads. He would make use of it on a hunting **fetish**, George had said. Maybe make one for both of them. And the Doctor had been furious, and now Isaacs would not let anyone come anymore to watch him work. Crazy George.

The Fire God rubbed his legs, feeling a tightening in the thigh muscles as breeze dried the sweat. In seventeen more seconds he would run again, cover the last mile down the mesa slope to where George would be waiting with his bicycle. Then he would go home and finish his homework.

He ran again, moving first at a slow jog and then faster as the stiffness left. Sweat again dampened the back of his sweat shirt, darkening the stenciled letters that said "Property of Zuñi Consolidated Schools." Under the angry red sky he ran, into the thickening darkness, thinking of crazy George, his oldest

....

site of the anthropologist's dig place where scientists dig in the ground to learn about people who lived there long ago

fetish object that is worshipped for its magical powers

and best friend. He thought of George collecting cactus buttons for the **doper** at the hippie commune, and eating them himself in search of visions, of George going to the old man at the edge of Zuñi to learn how to become a **sorcerer**, and how angry the old man had been, of George wanting to quit being a Navajo so he could be a Zuñi. George was certainly crazy, but George was his friend, and here now was his bicycle and George would be waiting.

The figure which stepped from behind the boulders in the red darkness was not George. It was a Salamobia, its round yellow-circled eyes staring at him. The Fire God stopped, opened his mouth, and found nothing to say. This was the Salamobia of the mole kiva, its mask painted the color of darkness. And yet it was not. The Fire God stared at the figure, the muscular body in the dark shirt, the bristling ruff of turkey feathers surrounding the neck, the black and empty eyes, the fierce beak, the plumed feathered topknot. Black was the color of the Mole Salamobia, but this was not the mask. He knew that mask. His mother's uncle was the **personifier** of the Mole Salamobia and the mask lived at a **shrine** in his mother's uncle's home. But if it was not the mask . . .

The Fire God saw then that the wand rising in the hand of this Salamobia was not of woven yucca. It glittered in the red light of the twilight. And he remembered that Salamobia, like all of the ancestor spirits which lived at the Zuñi masks, were visible only to members of the Sorcery Fraternity, and to those about to die.

....

doper person who does illegal drugs
sorcerer male witch
personifier person who wore the mask
shrine place devoted to a religious object

≫ **2** ≪

Monday, December 1, 12:20 P.M.

Lieutenant Joe Leaphorn was watching the fly. He should have been listening to Ed Pasquaanti, who, perched on a swivel chair behind the desk marked "Chief of Police, Zuñi" was talking steadily in a quick, precise voice. But Pasquaanti was discussing **the jurisdictional problem** and Leaphorn already understood both the problem and why Pasquaanti was talking about it. Pasquaanti wanted to make sure that Leaphorn and McKinley County Deputy Sheriff Cipriano ("Orange") Naranjo and State Policeman J. D. Highsmith understood that on the Zuñi reservation the Zuñi police would be **running the investigation.** And that was fine with Leaphorn. The sooner he got away from here, the happier he'd be. The fly had distracted him a moment or two earlier by landing on his notebook. It walked now, with the sluggishness of all winter-doomed insects, up the margin of the paper toward his finger. Would a Zuñi fly **deign to tread** upon Navajo skin? Leaphorn instantly regretted the thought. It represented a **slip back into the illogical hostility** he had been struggling against all morning—ever since he had been handed, at the Ramah chapter house, the

....

the jurisdictional problem who has the authority
running the investigation in charge of the search
deign to tread lower its standards and walk
slip back into the illogical hostility return to anger

message which had sent him over here.

Typical of the radio messages Leaphorn received from Shiprock, it said a little too little. Leaphorn was to drive over to Zuñi **without delay** to help find George Bowlegs, fourteen, a Navajo. Other details would be available from Zuñi police, with whom Leaphorn was **instructed** to cooperate.

The radioman at the Raman communications center grinned when he handed it over. "Before you ask," he said, "yes, this is all they said. And no, I don't know a damn thing about it."

"Well, hell," Leaphorn said. He could see how it would work. A thirty-mile drive over to Zuñi to find out that the kid had stolen something or other and had disappeared. But the Zuñis wouldn't know a damn thing about the boy. So then there would be the thirty-mile drive back to the Ramah reservation to find out where to look for him. And then . . . "You know anything about this George Bowlegs?" he asked.

The radioman knew about what Leaphorn had expected he would. He wasn't sure, but maybe the boy was the son of a guy named Shorty Bowlegs. Shorty had moved back from the Big Reservation after something went wrong with a woman he'd married over there around Coyote Canyon. This Shorty Bowlegs was a member of the High Standing House **clan**, and one of the boys of Old Woman Running. And once, after he had come back from Coyote Canyon, he had applied for **a land use allocation** with the grazing committee here. But then he had moved off somewhere. And maybe this was the wrong

....

without delay immediately

instructed told

clan group

a land use allocation permission to use land

man, anyway.

"O.K., then," Leaphorn said. "If anybody wants me, I'll be at the police station in Zuñi."

"Don't look so sour," the radioman said, still grinning. "I don't think the Zuñis' been initiating anybody into the Bow Society lately."

Leaphorn had laughed at that. Once, or so Navajos believed, initiates into the Zuñi Bow priesthood had been required to bring **a Navajo scalp**. He laughed, but his mood remained sour. He drove down N.M. 53 toward Zuñi a little faster than he should, the mood bothering him because he could find no logical reason to explain it. Why resent this assignment? The job that had taken him to Ramah had been **onerous** enough to make an interruption welcome. An old Singer had complained that he had given a neighbor woman eight hundred dollars to take into Gallup and make a down payment on a pickup truck, and the woman had spent his money. Some of the facts had been easy enough to establish. The woman had retrieved almost eight hundred dollars of her pawn from a Gallup shop on the **day in question** and she hadn't given any money to the car-lot owner. So it should have been simple, but it wasn't. The woman said the Singer owed her the money, and that the Singer was a witch, a Navajo Wolf. And then there was the question of **which side of the boundary fence** they'd been standing on when the money changed hands. If she was standing where she said she had been, they were on Navajo reservation land and under tribal-federal jurisdiction. But if they stood where the

....

a Navajo scalp the top part of a Navajo's head
onerous troublesome
day in question day she committed the crime
which side of the boundary fence whose land

Singer claimed, they were over on **nonreservation allocation land** and the case would probably be tried under the New Mexico embezzlement law. Leaphorn could think of no way to resolve that problem and ordinarily he would have welcomed even a temporary escape from it. But he found himself resenting this job—hunting a fellow Navajo **at the behest of** Zuñis.

Pasquaanti's voice rattled on. The fly took a tentative step toward Leaphorn's hard brown knuckle, then stopped. Leaphorn suddenly understood his mood. It was because he felt that Zuñis felt superior to Navajos. And he felt this because he, Joe Leaphorn, had once—a long time ago—had a Zuñi roommate during his freshman year at Arizona State about whom he had developed a silly **inferiority complex**. Therefore his present mood wasn't at all logical, and Leaphorn disliked illogic in others and detested it in himself. The fly walked around his finger and disappeared, upside down, under the notebook. Pasquaanti stopped talking.

"I don't think we're going to have any jurisdictional problems," Leaphorn said impatiently. "So why don't you **fill us in on** what we're working on?" It would have been more polite to let Pasquaanti set his own pace. Leaphorn knew it, and he saw in Pasquaanti's face that the Zuñi knew he knew it.

"Here's what we know so far," Pasquaanti said. He shuffled a Xeroxed page to each of them. "Two boys missing and a pretty good bet that one of them got cut."

Two boys? Leaphorn scanned the page quickly and then, abruptly interested, went back over every sentence carefully.

....

nonreservation allocation land New Mexico land
at the behest of because of an order from
inferiority complex feeling of being not as good
fill us in on tell us about

20

Two boys missing. Bowlegs and a Zuñi named Ernesto Cata, and the Cata boy's bicycle, and a "large" expanse of blood soaked into the ground where the bicycle had been left.

"It says here they're classmates," Leaphorn said. "But Bowlegs is fourteen and Cata is listed as twelve. Were they in the same grade?" Leaphorn wished instantly he'd not asked the question. Pasquaanti would simply remind them all that Bowlegs was a Navajo—thereby explaining **the gap in academic performance**.

"Both in the seventh grade," Pasquaanti said. "The Cata boy'd be thirteen in a day or two. They'd been close friends two, three years. Good friends. Everybody says it."

"No **trace** of a weapon?" Naranjo asked.

"Nothing," Pasquaanti said. "Just blood. The weapon could have been anything that will let the blood out of you. You never saw so much blood. But I'd guess it wasn't a gun. Nobody remembers hearing anything that sounded like a shot and it happened close enough to the village so *somebody* would have heard." Pasquaanti paused. "I'd guess it was something that chopped. There was blood sprayed on the needles of piñon there as well as all that soaked into the ground, so maybe something cut a major **artery** while he was standing there. Anyway, whoever it was must have taken the weapon with him."

"Whoever?" Leaphorn said. "Then you're not all that sure Bowlegs is the one?"

Pasquaanti looked at him, studying his face. "We're not sure of nothing," he said. "All we know is down there. The Cata boy

....

the gap in academic performance why Bowlegs did not do well in school

trace evidence, sign

artery vein that sends blood away from the heart

didn't come home last night. They went out looking for him when it got daylight and they found the blood where he left his bicycle. The Bowlegs kid had borrowed the bike and he was supposed to bring it back there to that meeting place they had. O.K.? So the Bowlegs boy shows up at school this morning, but when we find out about the borrowed bike and all and send a man over there to talk to him, he's gone. Turns out he got up during his social studies class and said something to the teacher about feeling sick and cut out."

"If he did the killing," Naranjo said, "you'd think he'd have run right after he did it."

"Course we don't know there *was* a killing yet," Pasquaanti said. "That could be animal blood. Lot of **butchering** going on now. People getting ready for all that cooking for Shalako."

"Unless maybe Bowlegs was smart enough to figure no one would suspect him unless he did run," Naranjo said. "So he came to school and then he **lost his nerve** and ran anyway."

"I don't think it got typed up there in the report, but the kids said Bowlegs was looking for Cata when he got to school, asking where he was and all," Pasquaanti said.

"**That could have been part of the act**," Leaphorn said. He was glad to find he was thinking like a cop again.

"I guess so," Pasquaanti said. "But remember he's just fourteen years old."

Leaphorn tapped the page. "It says here that Cata had gone out to run. What was it? Track team or something?"

The silence lasted maybe three seconds—long enough to

....

butchering animal killing

lost his nerve became nervous

That could have been part of the act Bowlegs could have been pretending to look for Cata

22

tell Leaphorn the answer wouldn't be the track team. It would be something to do with the Zuñi religion. Pasquaanti was deciding exactly how much he wanted them to know before he opened his mouth.

"This Cata boy had been selected to have a part in the religious ceremonials this year," Pasquaanti said. "Some of those ceremonials last for hours, the dancing is hard, and you have to be **in condition**. He was running every evening to keep in condition."

Leaphorn was remembering the Shalako ceremonial he'd attended a long time ago—back when he'd had a freshman Zuñi roommate. "Was Cata the one they call the Fire God?" he asked. "The one who is painted black and wears the spotted mask and carries the firebrand?"

"Yeah," Pasquaanti said. "Cata was Shulawitsi." He looked uncomfortable. "I don't imagine that has anything to do with this, though."

Leaphorn thought about it. Probably not, he decided. He wished he knew more about the Zuñi religion. But that wouldn't be his problem anyway. His problem would be finding George Bowlegs.

Pasquaanti was **fumbling through** a folder. "The only picture we have of the boys so far is the one in the school yearbook." He handed each of them a page of photos, two of the faces circled with red ink. "If we don't find them quick, we'll get the photographer to make us some **big blowups** off the negatives," he said. "We'll get copies of the pictures

....

in condition in good shape; physically fit
fumbling through looking at the papers inside
big blowups big pictures; enlargements

sent over to the sheriff's office and the state police, and over to the Arizona state police, too. And if we find out anything we'll **get the word to you** right away so you won't be wasting your time." Pasquaanti got up. "I'm going to ask Lieutenant Leaphorn to sort of concentrate on trying to find out where George Bowlegs got to. We'll be working on trying to find Ernesto and the bicycle, and anything else we can find out."

It occurred to Leaphorn that Pasquaanti, with his jurisdiction properly established, was not offering any advice about how to find Bowlegs. He was **presuming** that Naranjo and Highsmith and Leaphorn understood their jobs and knew how to do them.

"I'll need to know where Bowlegs lived, and if anybody's been there to see if he went home."

"It's about four miles out to where Shorty Bowlegs has his **hogan** and I'm going to have to draw you a little map," Pasquaanti said. "We went out, but we didn't learn anything."

Leaphorn's expression asked the question for him.

Pasquaanti looked slightly embarrassed. "Shorty was there. But he was too drunk to talk."

"O.K.," Leaphorn said. "Did you find any tracks around where you found the blood?"

"Lot of bicycle tracks. He'd been going there for months to start running. And then there was a place where somebody wearing **moccasins** or some sort of heelless shoes had been standing around. Looks like he waited quite a while. Found a place where he sat under the piñon there. Crushed down some

....

get the word to you tell you
presuming assuming
hogan Navajo house
moccasins soft, leather shoes

weeds. And then there was the tracks of Ernesto's track shoes. It's mostly rock in that place. **Hard to read anything.**"

Leaphorn was thinking that he might go to this spot himself, that he could find tracks where a Zuñi couldn't. Pasquaanti was looking at him, suspecting such thoughts. "You didn't find anything that told you much, then?" Leaphorn asked.

"Just that our boy Ernesto Cata had a lot of blood in him," Pasquaanti said. He smiled at Leaphorn, but the smile was **grim**.

....

Hard to read anything. It was hard to see any footprints.
grim not happy

BEFORE YOU MOVE ON...

1. **Character** Why does Ernesto Cata think that his friend George Bowlegs is crazy?
2. **Conflict** What is the problem that starts this story? Who is supposed to solve the problem?

LOOK AHEAD Read pages 26–37 to find out if George's brother, Cecil, tells Leaphorn any important information.

3

Monday, December 1, 3:50 P.M.

The tire blew about halfway back from Shorty Bowlegs's place, reconfirming Leaphorn's belief that days that begin badly tend to end badly. The road wound through the rough country behind Corn Mountain—nothing more than a seldom-used wagon track. One *could* follow it through the summer's growth of weeds and grama grass if one paid proper attention. Leaphorn hadn't. He had concentrated on **making some sense of** what little he had learned from Bowlegs instead of on his driving. And the left front wheel had slammed into a weed-covered pothole and ruptured its sidewall.

He set the jack under the front bumper. Bowlegs had been too drunk **for coherent conversation**. But apparently he had seen George this morning when the boy and his younger brother left on the long walk to catch the school bus. The elder Bowlegs didn't seem to have **the faintest** idea when George had returned to the hogan Sunday night. That could mean either that it was after Shorty had gone to sleep or that Shorty had been too drunk to notice.

Leaphorn pumped the jack handle, feeling irritated and

The tire blew The car had a flat tire
making some sense of understanding
for coherent conversation to talk
the faintest any

slightly sorry for himself. By now Highsmith would be cruising comfortably down Interstate 40, having filed his descriptions of George Bowlegs and Ernesto Cata **in the channels** which would assure that highway patrolmen would **eye** young Indian hitchhikers with suspicion. And Orange Naranjo would be back in Gallup and equally done with it once his report was circulated in the proper places. Pasquaanti would have given up on finding any tracks by now and would simply be waiting. There would be nothing much else to do in Zuñi. The **word** would have spread within an hour through every red stone home in the beehive village and across the reservation that one of the sons of Zuñi was missing and probably dead and that the Navajo boy who was always hanging around was wanted by the police. If any Zuñi saw George Bowlegs anywhere, Pasquaanti would know it fast.

The jack slipped on the slope of the pothole. Leaphorn cursed with feeling and eloquence, removed the jack, and began laboriously chipping out a firmer base in the rocky soil with the jack handle. The outburst of profanity had made him feel a little better. After all, what the sergeant and the deputy and the Zuñi cop were doing was all that it made any sense for them to do. If Bowlegs headed for Albuquerque or Phoenix or Gallup, or hung around Zuñi territory, he would almost certainly be picked up quickly and efficiently. If he **holed up** somewhere in Navajo country, that would be Leaphorn's problem—and it was nobody's fault that it was a much tougher one, solvable only by persistent hard work. Leaphorn reset the jack, reinserted the

....

in the channels with the police
eye look at
word information
holed up hid

handle, stretched his cramped muscles, and looked down the wagon track at the expanse of wooded mesas and broken canyon country stretching toward the southern horizon. He saw the beauty, the patterned cloud shadows, the red of the cliffs, and everywhere the blue, gold, and gray of dry country autumn. But soon the north wind would take the last few leaves and one cold night this landscape would change to solid white. And then George Bowlegs, if he was hiding somewhere in it, would be in trouble. He would survive easily enough until the snow came. There were dried berries and **edible roots** and rabbits, and a Navajo boy would know where to find them. But one day an end would come to the endless sunshine of the mountain autumn. An arctic storm front would bulge down out of western Canada, down the west slope of the Rockies. Here the **altitude** was almost a mile and a half above sea level and there was already hard frost in the mornings. With the first storm, the mornings would be **subzero**. There would be no way to find food with the snow blowing. On the first day, George Bowlegs would be hungry. Then he would be weak. And then he would freeze.

Leaphorn grimaced and turned back to the jack. It was then he saw the boy standing there shyly, not fifty feet away, waiting to be noticed. He recognized him instantly from the yearbook photograph. The same rounded forehead, the same wide-set, alert eyes, the same wide mouth. Leaphorn pumped the jack handle. "**Ya-ta-hey**," he said.

"Ya-ta-hey, uncle," the boy said. He had a book covered with

....

edible roots roots he could eat
altitude height of land
subzero extremely cold
Ya-ta-hey Hello (in Navajo)

butcher paper in his hand.

"You want to help change this wheel? I could use some help."

"O.K.," the boy said. "Give me the trunk key and I'll get the **spare**."

Leaphorn **fished** the keys out of his pocket, realizing now that this boy was too young to be George Bowlegs. He would be Cecil, the younger brother.

Cecil brought the spare while Leaphorn removed the last lug nuts. Leaphorn was thinking hard. He would be very careful.

"You're a *Navajo* policeman," the boy said. "I thought at first it was the Zuñi patrol car."

"The car belongs to the **Dinee**," Leaphorn said. "Just like you and I." Leaphorn paused, looking at Cecil. "And just like George, your brother." A flicker of surprise crossed the boy's face, and then it was **blank**.

"We are all of The People," Leaphorn said.

The boy glanced at him, silent.

"It would be a good thing if George talked to a Dinee policeman," Leaphorn said. He stressed the word "Dinee," which meant "The People."

"You're hunting him." The boy's voice was accusing. "You think like the Zuñis said at school that he ran away because he killed that Ernesto."

"I don't even know the Zuñi boy is dead. All I know now is what the Zuñi policeman told me," Leaphorn said. "I wonder

....

spare extra tire
fished took
Dinee Navajo people
blank without expression

what your brother would tell me."

Cecil said nothing. He **studied** Leaphorn's face.

"I don't think George ran away because he killed the Cata boy," Leaphorn said. "If he ran away maybe it was because he was afraid the Zuñi policeman would lock him in jail." Leaphorn removed the left front wheel and carefully fit the spare on the lug nuts, not looking at Cecil. "Maybe that was a smart thing to do. Maybe not. If he didn't kill the Cata boy, then running away wasn't smart. It made the Zuñis think maybe he was the one. But if he did kill the Cata boy, maybe it was smart and maybe it wasn't. Because probably they will catch him and then it will be worse for him. And if they don't catch him, he will have to run all the rest of his life." Leaphorn reached for the lug wrench, looking at Cecil now. "That is a bad way to live. It would be better to spend a few years in jail and **get it over with**. Or maybe spend some time in a hospital. If that boy is dead, and if George was the one who killed him, it was because there is something wrong inside his head. He needs to have it cured. The authorities would put him in a hospital instead of the jail."

The silence ticked away. A gust of breeze moved down the hillside, ruffling the grama grass. It was cold.

Cecil licked his lips. "George didn't run because he was afraid of the Zuñi police," he said. "That wasn't why."

"Why then, nephew?" Leaphorn asked.

"It was the kachina." The boy's voice was so **faint** that Leaphorn wasn't sure he had heard it. "He ran away from

....

studied looked carefully at

get it over with finish his punishment quickly

The silence ticked away. It was quiet for awhile.

faint quiet

30

the kachina."

"Kachina? What kachina?" It was a strange sensation, more than **an abrupt** change of subject; more like an unexpected **shift** from real to unreal. Leaphorn stared at Cecil. The word "kachina" had three meanings. They were the ancestor spirits of the Zuñi. Or the masks worn to impersonate these spirits. Or the small wooden dolls the Zuñis made to represent them. The boy wasn't going to say anything more. This kachina business was just **something that had come off his tongue**— something to avoid telling what he knew.

"I don't know its name," Cecil said finally. "It's a Zuñi word. But I guess it would be the same kachina that got Ernesto."

"Oh," Leaphorn said. He tested the tightness of the lug nuts, lowered the jack, giving himself time to think. He rested his hip on the **fender** and looked at Cecil Bowlegs. The crumpled sack that jutted from the boy's jacket pocket would be his lunch sack—empty now. What would Cecil find in that hogan to take to school for lunch?

"Did a kachina get Ernesto Cata? How did you find out?"

Cecil looked embarrassed.

The boy was lying. That was obvious. And no boy that age was good at it. Leaphorn had found that listening carefully to lies is sometimes very revealing of the truth. "Why would the kachina get after Ernesto? Do you know the reason?"

Cecil caught his lower lip between his teeth. He looked past Leaphorn, thinking.

"Do you know why George is running away from

....

an abrupt a sudden
shift change
something that had come off his tongue a lie
fender side of the car

this kachina?"

"I think it's the same reason," Cecil said.

"You don't know the reason, but whatever it is, it would make the kachina **go after** both of them?"

"Yeah," Cecil said. "I think that's the way it is."

Leaphorn no longer thought Cecil was lying. George must have told him all this.

"I guess, then, from what you tell me, that Ernesto and George must have done something that made the kachina mad."

"Ernesto did it. George just listened to him. Telling is what breaks the taboo and Ernesto told. George just listened." Cecil's voice was earnest, as if it was very important to him that no one think his brother had broken a Zuñi taboo.

"Told what?"

"I don't know. George said he didn't think he should tell me. But it was something about the kachinas."

Leaphorn pushed himself away from the fender and sat down on the dead grass, folding his legs in front of him. What he had to find out was fairly simple. Did George know the Cata boy was dead when George and Cecil left for school this morning? If he knew that, it would almost certainly mean that George had either killed Ernesto, or had seen him killed, or had seen the killer **disposing of** the body. But if he asked Cecil **straight out**, and the answer was negative, Leaphorn knew he would have to **discount** the answer. Cecil would lie to protect his brother. Leaphorn fished out his cigarettes. He didn't like what he was about to do. My job is to find George Bowlegs, he

---

go after hunt, chase
disposing of get rid of
straight out directly
discount ignore

told himself. It's important to find him. "Do you sometimes smoke a cigarette?' he asked Cecil. He **extended the pack**.

Cecil took one. "Sometimes it is good," he said.

"It's never good. It hurts the lungs. But sometimes it is necessary, and therefore one does it."

Cecil sat on a rock, inhaled deeply, and let the smoke trickle out of his nostrils. Obviously it wasn't his first experience with tobacco.

"You think Cata broke a taboo, and the kachina got Cata for doing it, and is after George." Leaphorn spoke thoughtfully. He exhaled a cloud of smoke. It hung blue in the still sunlight. "Do you know when George got home last night?"

"After I was asleep," Cecil said. "He was there when I woke up this morning, getting ready to catch the school bus."

"You boys like school better than I did," Leaphorn said. "When I was a boy, I would have told my daddy probably no school today because one of the students got killed yesterday. Maybe he'd let me stay home. **Worth trying**, anyway." The tone was casual, **bantering**, exactly right, he felt. Maybe it would **elicit an unguarded admission**, and maybe it wouldn't. If not, he'd simply try again. Leaphorn was a man of immense patience.

"I didn't know about it yet," Cecil said. "Not till we got to school." He was staring at Leaphorn. "They didn't find the blood until this morning." Cecil's expression said he was wondering how this policeman could have forgotten that, and then he knew Leaphorn hadn't forgotten. The boy's face was

....

extended the pack offered a cigarette

Worth trying I could ask him

bantering playful and friendly

elicit an unguarded admission make Cecil tell a secret

briefly angry, then simply **forlorn**. He looked away.

"To hell with it," Leaphorn said. "Look, Cecil. I was trying to **screw you around**. Trying to trick you into telling me more than you want to tell me. Well, to hell with that. He's your brother. You think about it and then you tell me just what you'd want a policeman to know. And remember, it won't be just me you're telling. I've got to pass it on—most of it, anyway—to the Zuñi police. So be careful not to tell me anything you think would hurt your brother."

"What do you want to know? Where George is? I don't know that."

"A lot of things. Mostly, a way to find George, because when I can talk to him he can give us all the answers. Like did he see what happened to Cata? Was he there? Did he do it? Did somebody else do it? But I can't talk to George until I figure out where he went. You say he didn't tell you this morning that something had happened to Cata. But he **gave you the idea** that a kachina was **after** both of them. What did he say?"

"It was kind of confused," Cecil said. "He was excited. I guess he borrowed Ernesto's bike after school and he took it back to where Ernesto was running and he was waiting there for Ernesto." Cecil stopped, trying to remember. "It was getting dark, and I guess it was then he saw the kachina coming. And he ran away from there and walked home. He didn't say it that way exactly, but that's what I think happened. When we got to school today, he was going to find out about the kachina."

"You didn't see George after he got off the bus?"

....

forlorn sad
screw you around trick you
gave you the idea made you think
after chasing

"No. He went looking for Ernesto."

"If you were me, where would you look for him?"

Cecil said nothing. He looked down at his shoes. Leaphorn noticed that the **sole** on the left one had split from the upper and they had been stuck together with some sort of grayish glue. But the glue hadn't held.

"O.K.," Leaphorn said. "Then has he got any other friends there at school? Anybody else who I should talk to?"

"No friends there at school," Cecil said. "They're Zuñis." He glanced at Leaphorn, to see if he understood. "They don't like Navajos," he said. "Just make jokes about us. Like **Polack jokes**."

"Just Ernesto? Everybody says Ernesto and George were friends."

"Everybody says George is kind of crazy," Cecil said. "It's because he wants to . . ." The boy stopped, hunting words. "He wants to do things, you know. He wants to try everything. One time he wanted to be a witch, and then he studied about Zuñi **sorcery**. And one time he was eating cactus buttons so he would have dreams. And Ernesto thought all that was fun, and he made George worse than he was about it. I don't think Ernesto was a friend. Not really a friend." Cecil's face was angry. "He was a goddam Zuñi," he said.

"How about anybody else? Anybody that might know anything."

"There's those white men who are doing all that digging for the arrowheads. George used to go there a lot and watch that

....

sole bottom
Polack jokes jokes about Polish people
sorcery magic

one man dig. Used to hang around there most of the summer and then after school started, too. Him and that Zuñi. But Ernesto stole something, I think, and they **ran 'em off**."

Leaphorn had noticed the anthropology site and had asked Pasquaanti about it. It was less than a mile from where the blood had been found.

"Like stole what? When did that happen?"

"Just the other day," Cecil said. "I think Ernesto stole some of that flint they dug up. I think it was arrowheads and stuff like that."

Leaphorn started to ask why they would want to steal flint artifacts but bit off the question. Why did boys steal anything? Mostly to see if they could **get away with it**.

"And then there's those **Belacani** living over in the old hogans behind Hoski Butte," Cecil said. "George liked that blond girl over there and she was trying to teach him to play the guitar, I think."

"White people? Who are these Belacani?"

"**Hippies**," Cecil said. "Bunch of them been living over there. They're raising some sheep."

"I'll talk to them," Leaphorn said. "Anyone else?"

"No," Cecil said. He hesitated. "You been to our place, just now. My father. Was he . . ." Embarrassment overcame the need to know.

"Yeah," Leaphorn said. "He'd been drinking some. But I

....

ran 'em off made them leave; chased them away
get away with it steal without getting caught
Belacani white people (in Navajo)
Hippies People who believe in peace and free love

think it'll be all right. I think he'll be asleep by the time you get home." And then he looked away from the pain and the shame in Cecil's face.

BEFORE YOU MOVE ON...

1. **Inference** Why does Leaphorn tell Cecil that he is a Dinee, or a Navajo, policeman?

2. **Summarize** What are 2 possible reasons someone might have killed Cata?

LOOK AHEAD Read pages 38–55 to find out what Dr. Reynolds and Ted Isaacs are trying to prove.

4

Monday, December 1, 4:18 P.M.

Ted Isaacs ran the shovel blade carefully into the dusty earth. The pressure on the heel of his hand told him that the resistance to the blade was a little light, that he was digging slightly above the high-calcium layer which Isaacs now knew—with absolute certainty—was the **Folsom floor**. He withdrew the blade and made a second stroke—a half-inch deeper—his hand now registering the feel of the metal sliding along the proper **strata**.

"Twenty," he said, dumping the earth on the pile on the sifter screen. He leaned the shovel against the wheelbarrow and began sorting the soft earth through the wire with a worn **trowel**. He worked steadily, and fast, pausing only to toss away clumps of grama grass roots and the tangles of tumbleweeds. Within three minutes nothing was left on the screen except an assortment of pebbles, small twigs, old rabbit droppings, and a large scorpion—its barbed tail waving in confused anger. Isaacs fished the scorpion off the wire with a stick and flicked it in the direction of his **horned lark**. The lark, a female, had been his only companion for the past two days, flirting around

----

Folsom floor layer of earth where he could find artifacts
strata layer
trowel small hand shovel
horned lark bird

the dig site feasting on such tidbits. Isaacs wiped the sweat with his sleeve and then sorted carefully through the pebbles. He was a tall, bony young man. Now the sun was low behind Corn Mountain and he worked hatless—the white skin high on his forehead contrasting sharply with the burned brown leather of his face. His hands worked with delicate speed, blunt, callused fingers **eliminating** most of the stones automatically, rejecting others after a quick exploratory touch, finally pausing with a chip no larger than a toenail clipping. This chip Isaacs examined, squinting in concentration. He put it into his mouth, cleaned it quickly with his tongue, spit, and reexamined it. It was a chip of agate flint—the third he had found this morning. He fished a jeweler's glass from the pocket of his denim shirt. Through the double lens, the chip loomed huge against the now massive ridges of his thumbprint. On one edge there was the scar he knew he would find—the **point of percussion**, the mark left a hundred centuries ago when a Folsom hunter had flaked it off whatever tool he had been making. The thought aroused in Isaacs a sense of excitement. It always had, since his very first dig as part of an undergraduate team—**an exhilarating sense of making a quantum leap backward through time**.

Isaacs stuffed the glass back in his pocket and extracted an envelope. He wrote "Grid 4 north, 7 west" on it in a small, neat hand, and dropped in the flake. It was then he noticed the white panel truck jolting up the ridge toward him.

"Crap," Isaacs said. He stared at the truck, hoping it would go away. It didn't. It kept bumping inexorably toward him,

....

eliminating throwing away

point of percussion place where it was hit

an exhilarating sense of making a quantum leap backward through time an exciting feeling of discovering something from a very long time ago

following the tracks his own truck-camper had left through the grama grass. And finally it stopped a polite fifty feet below the area marked by his network of white strings. Stopped gradually, avoiding the great cloud of dust which Dr. Reynolds in his **perpetual** hurry always produced when he drove his pickup up to the site.

The door of the **carryall bore a round seal** with a stylized profile of a buffalo, and the man who got out of it and was now walking toward Isaacs wore the same seal on the shoulder of his khaki shirt. The man had an Indian face. Tall, though, for a Zuñi, with a lanky, rawboned look. Probably a Bureau of Indian Affairs employee—which meant he could be anything from an Eskimo to an Iroquois. Whoever he was, he stopped several feet short of the white string marking the boundary of the dig.

"What can I do for you?" Isaacs said.

"Just looking for some information," the Indian said. "You have time to talk?"

"Take time," Isaacs said. "Come on in."

The Indian made his way carefully across the network of strings, **skirting** the grids where the topsoil had already been removed. "My name's Leaphorn," he said. "I'm with the Navajo Police."

"Ted Isaacs." They shook hands.

"We're looking for a couple of boys," Leaphorn said. "A Navajo about fourteen named George Bowlegs and a twelve-year-old Zuñi named Ernesto Cata. I understand they **hang around** here a lot."

....

perpetual constant
carryall bore a round seal van had a picture
skirting walking around; avoiding
hang around visit

"They did," Isaacs said. "But not lately. I haven't seen them since . . ." He paused, remembering the scene, Reynolds' yell of outrage and anger and Cata running from Reynolds' pickup as if hell itself **pursued** him. The memory was a mixture of amusement and regret. It had been funny, but he missed the boys and Reynolds had **made it clear enough** in his direct way that he didn't think much of Isaacs' judgment in letting them hang around. ". . . not since last Thursday. Most afternoons they'd come by after school," Isaacs said. "Sometimes they'd stay around until dark. But the last few days . . ."

"Have any idea why they haven't been back?"

"We ran 'em off."

"Why?"

"Well," Isaacs said. "This is a research site. Not the best place in the world for a couple of boys to be **horsing around**."

Leaphorn said nothing. The silence stretched. Time ticking silently away made Isaacs nervous, but the Indian seemed unaware of it. He simply waited, his eyes black and patient, for Isaacs to say more.

"Reynolds caught them **screwing around** in his truck," Isaacs said, resenting the Indian for making him say it.

"What did they steal?"

"Steal? Why, nothing. Not that I know of. They didn't take anything. One of 'em was at Dr. Reynolds' truck and Reynolds yelled at him to get the hell away from his stuff and they ran away."

"Nothing missing?"

....

pursued chased
made it clear enough told him
horsing around playing
screwing around playing

41

"No. Why are you looking for them?"

"They're missing," Leaphorn said. Again the silence, the Indian's face thoughtful. "You're digging up **artifacts** here, I guess," he said. "Could they have gotten off with any of that stuff?"

Isaacs laughed. "**Over my dead body**," he said. "Besides, I would have missed it." The very thought made him nervous. He felt an urge to check, to hold the envelope marked "Grid 17 north, 23 west," to feel the shape of the broken lance point under his fingers, to know it was safe.

"You're absolutely sure, then? Could they have stolen anything at all?"

"Reynolds thought they might have got something out of his toolbox, I think, because he checked it. But nothing was gone."

"And no artifacts missing? Not even chips?"

"No way," Isaacs said. "I keep what I find in my shirt pocket here." Isaacs tapped the envelopes. And when I **knock off at dark** I lock it up in the camper. Why do you think they stole something?"

The Indian didn't seem to hear the question. He was looking toward Corn Mountain. Then he shrugged. "I heard they did," he said. "What are you digging here? Some sort of Early Man site?"

The question surprised Isaacs. "Yeah. It was a Folsom hunting camp. You know about the Folsom culture?"

"Some," Leaphorn said. "I studied a little **anthropology**

....

artifacts things made by people from long ago
Over my dead body I would never allow it
knock off at dark stop working for the day
anthropology history of early humans

at Arizona State. They didn't know much about Folsom then, though. Didn't know where he came from, or what happened to him."

"How long since you studied?"

"Too long," Leaphorn said. "I've forgotten most of it."

"You heard of Chester Reynolds?"

"I think he wrote one of my textbooks."

"Probably that was *Paleo-Indian Cultures in North America*. It's still **a standard**. Anyway, Reynolds worked out a set of maps of the way this part of the country looked back at the end of the last Ice Age—back when it was raining so much. From that he worked out the **game migration routes** at the very end of the Pleistocene period. You know. Where you'd find the mastodons and ground sloths and the saber-tooth cats and the long-horn bison, because of surface water and climate when this country started drying up. And from that he worked out the methods for calculating where the Folsom hunters were likely to have their hunting camps. That's what this was." Isaacs gestured across the gridwork of strings **waffling** the grassy ridge. "That flat place down there was a lake then. Folsom could sit up here on his haunches and see everything that came to water—either at the lake or north toward the Zuñi Wash."

Isaacs accepted a cigarette from Leaphorn. He sat on the frame of the sifter screen, looking tired and excited. And he talked. He talked as a naturally friendly man will talk when confronted—after days of **enforced silence**—with a good listener. He talked of how Reynolds had found this site and

....

a standard used often in classes

game migration routes paths that animals traveled

waffling making a pattern across

enforced silence not talking to anyone

a dozen others. And of how Reynolds had given the sites to selected **doctoral candidates**, arranged foundation grants to **finance** the work. He talked of Reynolds' modification theory—which would solve one of the great mysteries of American anthropology.

Leaphorn, who had always been fascinated by the unexplained, remembered the mystery from Anthropology 127. Folsom hunting camps had been found all over the central and southwestern states—their occupancy generally dating from as early as twelve thousand to as late as nine thousand years ago. During this era at the tag end of the Ice Age they seemed to have had this immense expanse of territory to themselves. They followed the bison herds, living in small camps where they chipped their lance points, knives, hide scrapers, and other tools from flint. These lance points **were their trademark**. They were leaf-shaped, small, remarkably thin, their faces fluted like bayonets, their points and cutting edges shaped by an unusual technique called "pressure flaking." Making such a point was difficult and **time consuming**. Other Stone Age people, later and earlier, made larger, cruder points, quick and easy to chip out and no less efficient at killing. But Folsom stuck to his beautiful but difficult design century after century and left anthropology with a puzzle. Was the lance point part of a ritual religion—its shape a magic offering to the spirit of the animals that fed Folsom with their meat? When the glaciers stopped melting, and the great rain ended, and the country dried, and the animal herds diminished, and survival became

....

doctoral candidates graduate students
finance pay for
were their trademark made them unique
time consuming took a lot of time

44

a very **chancy** thing, Folsom camps disappeared from the earth. Had Folsom Man been trapped by this time-consuming ritualism which delayed his **adaptation** to changing conditions and caused his **extinction**? Whatever the reason, he vanished. There was a gap when the Great Plains seem to have been virtually empty of men, and then different hunting cultures appeared, killing with long, heavy lance points and using different stone-working techniques.

"Yeah," Isaacs said. "That's about the way the books explain it. But thanks to Reynolds, they're going to have to rewrite all those books."

"You going to prove something else happened?"

"Yeah," Isaacs said. "We damn sure are." He lit another cigarette, puffed nervously. "Let me tell you what those bastards did. Two years ago, when Reynolds started working on this, he read a paper on his theory at the anthro convention and some of those stuffy old academic bastards walked out on him." Isaacs snorted. "Got up and walked right out of the general assembly session." He laughed. "Nobody's done that since the physical anthropologists walked out on the paper announcing the original Folsom discovery, and that was back in 1931."

"Pretty serious insult, I guess," Leaphorn said.

"The worst kind. I wasn't there, but I heard about it. They say Reynolds was ready to kill somebody. He's not used to that kind of treatment and he's not the kind of man you **push on**. They said he told some of his friends there that he'd make those people accept his theory if it took the rest of his life."

....

chancy difficult
adaptation ability to adjust
extinction complete disappearance
push on want to anger

"What's the Reynolds theory?"

"In brief, Folsom Man didn't die out. He adapted. He began making a different kind of lance point—some of those that **we've been crediting** to entirely different cultures. And, by God, we're going to prove it right here." Isaacs' voice was exultant.

It seemed to Leaphorn a hard case to prove. "Any chance of talking to Reynolds? Will he be back?"

"He's coming in this evening," Isaacs said. "Come on down to the camper. You can wait for him there, and I'll show you what we're finding."

The camper was parked amid a cluster of junipers—a plywood box of a cabin built on the bed of a battered old Chevy pickup truck. The inside was fitted with a narrow bunk, a linoleum-topped worktable, a small pantry, and an array of metal filing cabinets on one of which sat a portable butane cooking burner. Isaacs unlocked a cabinet, **extracted a tray of grimy** envelopes, counted them carefully, and then put all but one back. He motioned Leaphorn to the only stool and opened the envelope. He poured its contents carefully into his hand and then extended his open palm to Leaphorn. In it lay four chips of flint and a flat rectangle of pink stone. It was perhaps three inches long, an inch wide, and a half-inch thick.

"It's the butt end of a lance point," Isaacs said. "The type we call 'parallel flaked'—the type we always thought was made by a culture that **followed** Folsom." He pushed it with a finger. "Notice it's made out of **petrified wood**—silicified bamboo, to

....

we've been crediting to we thought were made by

extracted a tray of grimy took out some dirty

followed existed after

petrified wood wood that has become hard like stone

be exact. And notice these chips are the same stuff. And now"—he tapped the side of the stone with a fingernail—"notice that it isn't finished. He was still smoothing off this side when the tip **snapped** off."

"So," Leaphorn said slowly, "that means he was making it up there at your Folsom hunting camp and that he didn't just come along and drop it. But he still could have been making it a couple of thousand years after the Folsoms were gone."

"It was on the same stratum of earth," Isaacs said. "That's interesting, but in this sort of formation it doesn't prove anything. What's more interesting is this. There isn't any of this silicified bamboo anywhere near here. The only **deposit** we know of is over in the Galisteo Basin south of Santa Fe—a couple of hundred miles. Around here there's plenty of good flint—schist and chalcedony and other good stuff not half a mile from here. It's easy to shape, but it's not pretty. The other cultures used what was **handy and to hell with** how it looked. Folsom would find himself a quarry of clear, fancy-colored stuff and carry chunks of it all over the country to make his lance points." Isaacs pulled another envelope out of the file. "One more thing," he said. He emptied about a dozen flakes of pinkish stone into his palm and extended it. "These are pressure flakes. Typical and unmistakable **workshop debris** from a Folsom camp. And they're out of the same silicified petrification."

Leaphorn raised his eyebrows.

"Yeah," Isaacs said. "That gets to be quite a coincidence,

----

snapped broke
deposit place to find this kind of bamboo
handy and to hell with available and did not care
workshop debris leftover pieces

doesn't it? That two different bunches of hunters, two thousand years apart, would work the same quarry and then carry the stuff two hundred miles to work on it."

"I think you might call that real fine **circumstantial evidence**," Leaphorn said.

"And we're going to find enough of it so they'll have to believe it," Isaacs said. "I'm sure it happened here. The date's right. Our geologist tells us that high calcium layers were only formed about nine thousand years ago. So these were very late Folsoms." Isaacs' eyes were looking at a scene very distant in time. "There weren't many left. They were starving. The glaciers were long gone and the rains had stopped and the game herds were going fast. It was getting hotter, and the desert was spreading, and the culture they had lived by for three thousand years was failing them. They had to make a big kill at least every four or five days. If they didn't, they'd be too weak to hunt and they'd die. There just wasn't enough time anymore to make those fancy points that broke so easily." Isaacs glanced at Leaphorn. "Want some coffee?"

"Fine."

Isaacs began preparing the pot. Leaphorn tried to guess his age. Late twenties, he thought. No older than that, although his face sometimes had a **wizened**, old-man look about it. That was partly from the weathering. But something had **aged him**. Isaacs was conscious, Leaphorn had noticed earlier, of his teeth. They **were slightly buck**, and they protruded a little, and Isaacs called attention to them with an unconscious habit:

....

circumstantial evidence helpful proof
wizened wise
aged him made him look older
were slightly buck too big

he often had his hand to his face, shielding them. Now with the pot on the fire, he leaned against the wall, looking at Leaphorn. "It's always been presumed that they couldn't adapt so they died. That's **the textbook dogma**. But it's wrong. They were human, and smart; they had the intelligence to appreciate beauty and the intelligence to adapt."

Through the small window over the burner Leaphorn could see the red flare of the sunset. Red as blood. And was that blood under the piñon tree the blood of Ernesto Cata? And if so, what had happened to his body? And where under that garish evening sky could George Bowlegs be? But **there was no possible profit in pondering that question now**.

"I wonder, though," Leaphorn said. "Would changing your lance point make that much difference?"

"Probably not, by itself," Isaacs said. "But quite a bit. I can make a very rough version of a Folsom point in two or three hours on the average. They're so thin that you break a lot— and so did the Folsom Men. But you can whack out a big parallel-flaked point in maybe twenty minutes, and it's just as good as the ones Stone Age man used."

Isaacs fished a box of sugar cubes and a vacuum bottle cup out of a drawer and put them on the table beside Leaphorn. "We think he developed the Folsom point with all that symmetry in it as a sort of **ritual offering** to the animal spirit. Made it just as beautiful as he could make it. You're a Navajo. You know what I mean."

"I know," Leaphorn said. He was remembering a snowy

....

the textbook dogma what the textbooks always say
there was no possible profit in pondering that question now it was pointless to think about that now
ritual offering gift

morning on the Lukachukai plateau, his grandfather touching the barrel of his old **30-30** with sacred pollen, and then the chant—the old man's clear voice calling to the spirit of the male deer to make this hunt for the winter's meat right and proper and **in tune** with natural things; giving it the beauty of the Navajo Way.

"Reynolds figured—and he's right—that if Folsom was willing to change his lance point, he'd be willing to adapt in every other way. Under the old way, they'd be sitting in camp all day **turning out** maybe five or six of those fluted points, and maybe breaking ten or twelve to make a kill. They couldn't afford that anymore."

"Couldn't afford the beauty." Leaphorn laughed. "I went to a Bureau of Indian Affairs high school that had a sign in the hall. It said 'Tradition Is the Enemy of Progress.' The word was give up the old ways or die." He didn't mean it to sound bitter, but Isaacs gave him a **quizzical** look.

"By the way," Isaacs said. "Have you asked the people over at Jason's Fleece about those boys?"

"Jason's Fleece? Is that the hippie place?"

"They hung around there some," Isaacs said. "If they ran away from home, maybe they're over there. There's a girl over there that's a good friend of theirs. Nice girl named Susanne. The boys liked her."

"I'll go talk to her," Leaphorn said.

"That Bowlegs boy's a funny kid," Isaacs said. "He's sort of a mystic. Interested in magic and witchcraft and all that sort of

....

30-30 rifle
in tune in agreement
turning out making, creating
quizzical curious

thing. One time he was looking bad and I asked him about it and he said he was **fasting** so that **his totem** would talk to him. Wanted to see visions, I think. And one time they asked me if I could get them any **LSD**, and if I'd ever been on an acid trip."

"Could you?"

"Hell, no," Isaacs said. "Anyway, I wouldn't. That stuff's risky. Another thing, if it helps any." Isaacs laughed. "George was studying to be a Zuñi." He laughed again and shook his head. "George is sort of crazy."

"You mean studying their religion?"

"He said Ernesto was going to get him initiated into the Badger Clan."

"Could that happen?"

"I don't know," Isaacs said. "I doubt it. I think it's like a fish saying it's going to become a bird. The only time I ever heard of such a thing was back at the end of the nineteenth century when they adopted an anthropologist named Frank Cushing into the tribe."

Outside there was a sound of a motor whining in second gear—driving too fast over the bumpy track.

"Reynolds?"

Isaacs laughed. "That's the way the silly bastard drives."

Reynolds was not what Leaphorn had expected. Leaphorn had expected, he realized, **sort of a reincarnation of** the stooped, white-haired old man who had taught Leaphorn's cultural anthropology section at Arizona State. The typical scholar. Reynolds was medium-sized and medium everything.

....

fasting not eating for a long time

his totem the sacred object that represents his clan

LSD illegal drugs

sort of a reincarnation of someone who looked like

Perhaps fifty, but hard to **date**. Brown hair turning gray in spots, a round, cheerful face with the field anthropologist's leathery complexion. Only his eyes set him apart. They were notable eyes. Protected by a heavy brow ridge above and a lump of cheekbone below, they stared from their sockets with sharp, unblinking bright blue alertness. They gave Leaphorn, during the brief handshake of introduction, the feeling that everything about his face was being memorized. And a moment later they were studying with equal intensity the chips Isaacs had found that day. Joe Leaphorn, Navajo policeman, had been **sorted and stored out of the way**.

"Which grid?" Reynolds asked.

Isaacs touched three fingers to the map. "These."

"Washed down. Old erosion. See any of them in place?"

"Got 'em off the sifter screen," Isaacs said.

"You noticed they're silicated. Same stuff as the parallel-flaked?"

"Right."

"You're not missing anything?"

"I never do."

"I know you don't." Reynolds favored Isaacs with a glance that included fondness, warmth, and approval. It developed in a second into a smile that transformed Reynolds' leathery face into a statement of intense affection, and from that, in the same second, into **sheer, undiluted** delight.

"By God," he said. "By God, it really looks good. Right?"

"Very good, I think," Isaacs said. "I think this is going

....

date figure out how old he was

sorted and stored out of the way studied and forgotten

sheer, undiluted pure

to be it."

"Yes," Reynolds said. "I think so." He was staring at Isaacs. "Nothing's going wrong with this dig. You understand that? It is going to be done exactly right." Reynolds spaced the words, spitting each one out.

A good hater, Leaphorn thought. Maybe a little crazy. Or maybe just a genius.

Reynolds' gaze now included Leaphorn, the bright blue eyes checking their memory. "Mr. Isaacs is one of the three or four best field men in the United States," he said. The smile clicked on and off, the leather turned hard. "What Mr. Isaacs is doing here is going to make some stubborn people face the truth."

"I wish you luck," Leaphorn said.

Isaacs' face had done something Leaphorn wouldn't have believed possible. It **had assumed an expression of** embarrassed pleasure and managed to flush red through the sunburn. It made Isaacs look about ten years old.

"Mr. Leaphorn is looking for a couple of boys," he said. "He stopped by to ask if I'd seen them."

"Was one of them that Zuñi kid that was screwing around my truck?" Reynolds asked. "The one that ran off when I yelled at him?"

"That's the one," Leaphorn said. "I'd heard they stole something here."

Reynolds' bright eyes **flicked** instantly to Isaacs. "Did they steal something?"

"No," Isaacs said. "I told him that. Nothing's missing."

....

had assumed an expression of showed
flicked looked

Reynolds was still staring at Isaacs. "Were you letting two of them hang around here? I only saw one."

"The Zuñi boy and a Navajo named George Bowlegs," Leaphorn said. "They're friends and they're both gone. Did they steal something from you, Dr. Reynolds?"

"That Zuñi boy was poking around my truck. But nothing was missing. I don't think he stole anything. Frankly, I ran him off because it was beginning to look like this is a critically important site." Reynolds glanced at Isaacs. "It's damn sure no place to have **unauthorized persons underfoot**—especially not children."

"Was there anything in the pickup they might have stolen? Anything valuable?"

Reynolds thought about it. Impatience flashed across his face and was gone. "Is it important?"

"Those boys are missing. We think one of them was hurt. We need to know why they disappeared. Might help figure out where they are."

"Let's look, then," Reynolds said.

Outside the red sky was fading into darkness, and the early stars were **out**. Reynolds fished a flashlight out of the glovebox of a green GMC pickup. He checked the remaining contents— **a hodgepodge** of maps, small tools, and notebooks. "Nothing missing here," he said.

It took a little longer to check the toolbox welded behind the cab. Reynolds sorted carefully through the clutter—pliers, wire cutters, geologist's pick, hand ax, a folding trenching shovel,

....

unauthorized persons underfoot people who are not part of the dig nearby

out visible

a hodgepodge a collection; an assortment

and a dozen other **odds and ends**. "There's a hammer missing, I think. No. Here it is." He closed the box. **"All accounted for."**

"On the day you ran the boys off, did you have any artifacts in the truck?"

"Artifacts?" Reynolds was facing the sunset. It gave his skin a redness. The blue eyes memorized Leaphorn again.

"Arrowheads, lance points, anything like that?"

Reynolds thought about the question. "By God, I did. Had my box with me. But why would they want to steal a piece of rock?"

"I heard one of the boys stole an arrowhead," Leaphorn said. "Was anything missing from the box?"

Reynolds' laugh was more a snort. "You can be damned sure there wasn't. That box had stuff in it from all eight of the digs I'm watching. Nothing very important, but stuff we're working on. If a single flake was taken out of there, I'd know it. It's all there." He frowned. "Who told you he'd stolen some artifacts?"

"It's thirdhand," Leaphorn said. "The Navajo boy has a little brother. He told me."

"That's **funny**," Reynolds said.

Leaphorn said nothing. But he thought, Yes, that's very funny.

....

odds and ends things
"All accounted for." "All my things are here."
It's thirdhand Someone else told me
funny strange, odd

BEFORE YOU MOVE ON...

1. **Summarize** Reread page 46. Scientists thought that the Folsom Man died out. What is Reynolds's theory?

2. **Conclusions** Why does Leaphorn think it is strange that Cecil says one of the boys stole an artifact?

LOOK AHEAD Read pages 56–71 to find out who is following Leaphorn.

> **5** <

Monday, December 1, 8:37 P.M.

The moon now hung halfway up the sky, the yellow of its rising gone and its face turned to scarred white ice. It was a winter moon. Under it, Leaphorn was cold. He sat in the shadow of the rimrock watching the commune which called itself Jason's Fleece. The cold seeped through Leaphorn's uniform jacket, through his shirt and undershirt, and touched the skin along his ribs. It touched his calves above his boottops, and his thighs where the cloth of his trouser legs stretched **taut** against the muscles, and the backs of his hands, which gripped the metal of his binoculars. In a moment, Leaphorn intended to deal with the cold. He would get up and climb briskly down to the commune below him and learn there whatever it was possible for him to learn. But now he ignored the discomfort, concentrating in his orderly fashion on this minor phase of the job of finding George Bowlegs.

A less precise man by now would have **written off as wasted effort the mile walk** from the point where he had parked his carryall and the climb to this high point overlooking the commune. It didn't occur to Leaphorn to do so. He had

....

taut tight

written off as wasted effort the mile walk thought it was a waste of time to walk a mile

come here because his hunt for George Bowlegs logically led him to the commune. And before he entered it, he would study it. The chance that Bowlegs was hiding there seemed to Leaphorn **extremely slight**. But the chance existed and the **operating procedure** of Lieutenant Joe Leaphorn in such cases was to minimize the risk. Better spend whatever effort was required to examine the ground than chance losing the boy again by carelessness.

At the moment Leaphorn was examining, through the magnification of the binocular lenses, a denim jacket. The jacket hung on the corner post of a brush arbor beside a hogan some two hundred yards below where Leaphorn sat. The hogan was a neat octagon of logs built as the Navajo Way instructed, its single entrance facing the point of sunrise and a smoke hole in the center of the roof. Behind it Leaphorn could see a plank shed and behind the shed a pole corral that contained **huddled** sheep—probably about twenty. Leaphorn presumed the sheep belonged to the occupants of the commune, who currently numbered four men and three women. The allotment of land on which the sheep grazed belonged to Frank Bob Madman and the hogan, from which a thin plume of smoke now rose into the cold moonlight, belonged by Navajo tradition to the ghost of Alice Madman.

Leaphorn had learned this, and considerably more, by stopping at a hogan about four miles up the wagon track. With the young Navajo couple who lived there he had discussed the weather, the **sagging market** for wool, a Tribal Council

....

extremely slight not likely
operating procedure strategy, approach
huddled a group of
sagging market low demand

proposal to invest Navajo funds in the construction of livestock ponds, the couple's newborn son, and—finally—the group of Belacani who lived in the hogan down the wagon track. He had been told that Frank Bob Madman had abandoned the hogan almost three years before. Madman had gone to Gallup to buy salt and had returned to find that his wife of many years had died in his absence. ("She'd had a little stroke before," Young Wife said. "Probably had a big one this time.") There had been no one there to move Alice Madman out of the hogan so that her ghost—at the moment of death—might escape for its **eternity of wandering**. Therefore the **chindi** had been caught in the hogan. Madman had got a Belacani rancher over near Ramah to bury the body under rocks. He had knocked a hole in one wall and boarded up the smoke hole and the entrance, as was **customary** with a death hogan, to keep the ghost from bothering people. These duties performed, Madman had taken his wagon and his sheep, and left. Young Wife believed he had gone back to his own clan, the Red Foreheads, somewhere around Chinle. And then, a year ago last spring, the Belacani had arrived. There had been sixteen of them in a school bus and a Volkswagen van. They had moved into the Madman place, living in the death hogan and in two big tents. And then more had arrived until, by the end of summer, thirty-five or forty had lived there.

The number had declined during the winter, and in the coldest part of the year, in the very middle of the Season When the Thunder Sleeps, there had been another death in the hogan of the ghost of Alice Madman. The population had **stabilized**

....

eternity of wandering wandering that lasts forever
chindi spirit (in Navajo)
customary commonly done
stabilized stayed the same

during the spring and declined sharply again with the present autumn, until only four men and three women were left.

"The death?" Leaphorn asked. "Who was it? How did it happen?"

It had been a young woman, a very fat girl, a very quiet girl, sort of ugly. Somebody had said Ugly Girl had something wrong with her heart. Young Wife, however, thought it was too much heroin, or maybe the ghost of Alice Madman.

"Some of them were on **horse** then," Young Husband said. "Probably she **got an overdose** of the stuff. That's what we heard." Young Husband shrugged. He had spent twelve months with the First Cav in Vietnam. Neither heroin nor death impressed him. He discussed these whites with an impersonal interest tinged with amusement, but with the detailed knowledge of neighbors common to those who live where fellow humans are scarce. In general, Young Husband rated the residents of Jason's Fleece as generous, ignorant, friendly, bad mannered but well intentioned. On the positive side of the balance, they provided a source of free rides into Ramah, Gallup, and once even to Albuquerque. On the negative, they had **contaminated the spring above the Madman place with careless defecation** last summer, and had started a fire which burned off maybe fifty acres of pretty good sheep graze, and didn't know how to take care of their sheep, which meant they might let scabies, or some disease, get started in the flock. Yes, the visitors had included a Navajo boy who sometimes came by himself and sometimes came with a Zuñi boy.

....

horse heroin; illegal drugs

got an overdose had taken too much

contaminated the spring above the Madman place with careless defecation polluted the water near the Madman house by using it as a toilet

The other visitors were Belacani, mostly young, mostly long-haired. Young Wife was both amused and curious. What were they after? What were any of them after?

"They call their place Jason's Fleece," Leaphorn said. "Do you know the story about that? It's a hero story, like our story of the Monster Slayer and Born of Water, the twins who go to find the Sun. In the whiteman story Jason was a hero who hunted across the world for a golden fleece. Maybe it stood for money. I think it was supposed to stand for whatever it is people have to find to live happy."

"I heard of it," Young Husband said. "Supposed to be a sheepskin covered up with gold." He laughed. "I think you're more likely to find scabies on the sheep they're raising."

Leaphorn smiled slightly at the **recollection**, stared at the denim jacket, and decided the jacket looked too large to be the one Bowlegs was wearing when he left school. He **shifted his field of vision** slowly, past the thin plume of vapor rising from the smoke hole of the hogan, past the plank shed, past the brush arbor, then back again. There was a table under the arbor, partly in darkness. On it, cooking utensils reflected spots of moonlight. Beyond it something in the darkness which might be a saddle and something hanging which could only be a deer carcass. Leaphorn examined it. Something at the corner of his vision **tugged at** his attention. The shape of a shadow **contradicting** his memory of the way the shadows had been formed under this arbor. He shifted the binoculars slightly. Projected onto the hard bare earth behind the hogan

....

recollection thought, memory
shifted his field of vision looked around
tugged at got
contradicting that was different from

by the slanting light from the moon was the shadow of the pole which held up this corner of the shelter, and the shadow of part of the table, and beside that the shadow of a pair of legs. Someone was standing under the **arbor**. The shadow of the legs was motionless. Leaphorn frowned at it. The young neighbors had said only seven Belacani lived here now. He had seen two men and two women drive away in the school bus. He had seen one man and one woman—Susanne, judging from the description he had of her from Isaacs—go into the hogan. He had presumed the remaining man was also inside. Was this him standing so silently under the arbor? But why would he stand there in the icy moonlight? And how had he got there without Leaphorn seeing him? As he considered this, the figure moved. With birdlike swiftness it **darted out of** the arbor to the side of the hogan, disappearing into the shadow. It crouched, pressed against the logs. **What the devil was it doing?** Listening? It seemed to be. And then the figure straightened, its head moving upward into the slanting moonlight. Leaphorn sucked in his breath. The head was a bird's. Round, jaylike feather plumes thrusting backward, a long, narrow sandpiper's beak, a bristling ruff of feathers where the human neck would be. The head was round. As it turned away from profile, Leaphorn saw round eyes ringed with yellow against the black. He was seeing the staring, expressionless face of a kachina. Leaphorn felt the hairs bristling at the back of his neck. What was it his roommate had said of these spirits of the Zuñi dead? That they danced forever under a lake in Arizona; he remembered

---

arbor shadow of the roof
darted out of ran quickly from
What the devil was it doing? What was it doing?

that. The man-bird was moving again, away from the hogan to disappear through the darkness among the **piñons**. "The way it's told," he heard the roommate's voice saying, "they're invisible. But you can see them if you're about to die."

....

piñons pine trees

Monday, December 1, 9:11 *P.M.*

The girl named Susanne spoke with a slight stammer. It caused her to pause before each sentence—her oval, freckled face assuming a split second of earnest concentration before she **shaped** the first word. At the moment she was saying that maybe George Bowlegs was simply ditching school, that George sometimes **played hooky** to go deer hunting, that probably he was doing this now.

"Maybe that's so," Leaphorn said. He felt an amused attraction to this girl. She would be better at it someday, perhaps, but she would never be one of those who developed a skill at **deception**. He let the silence stretch. The blanket hanging against the log wall of the hogan opposite him was a good Two Gray Hills weave worth maybe three hundred dollars. Had Frank Bob Madman left it behind when this hogan was abandoned to its **malevolent** ghost? Or had these young Belacani bought it somewhere and brought it with them? The man called Halsey moved very slightly in his rocking chair, back and forth, his face hidden, except for the forehead, behind the black binding of a book. Halsey's boots were dirty, but they

....

shaped said
played hooky skipped school
deception lying
malevolent evil

were very good boots. Halsey interested Leaphorn. Where had he come from? And what did he hope to find here where the whiteman had never before found anything?

"Anyway," Susanne said, "I'm d-d-d-dead sure he didn't do anything to Ernesto. They were like brothers."

"I heard that," Leaphorn said. "Ted Isaacs told me—"

The young man with the shaved head said, *"No!"* The word was loud, startled, obviously not addressed to anything Leaphorn had been saying. It was the first word Leaphorn had heard the man speak. ("This is Otis," Susanne had said. "He's sick today." And Otis had turned glittering, unfocused eyes toward Leaphorn, staring up from the mattress on the hogan floor, saying nothing. It was not an unfamiliar look. Leaphorn had seen it in jail **drunk tanks**, in hospital wards, produced by wine and marijuana, by alcohol and **peyote buttons**, by the delirium of high fever, by LSD, by the venom of a rattlesnake bite.)

"No," Otis said again, more softly this time, simply confirming his rejection of some inner vision.

Susanne put her hand on the pale, bony arch of Otis's bare foot. "It's O.K., Oats," she said. "It's cool now. No problem."

Halsey leaned forward in his rocking chair, his face emerging past the book. He studied Otis and then glanced at Leaphorn, eyes curious. ("This is Halsey," Susanne had said. "He sort of **holds this place together**." Under his mustache Halsey grinned, challenging and combative, and extended his hand. "I never met a Navajo **fuzz** before," Halsey had said.)

....

drunk tanks cells where drunk people are kept
peyote buttons illegal drugs from a cactus
holds this place together manages this place
fuzz police officer

Whatever form Otis's nightmare took, it left his face drawn and bloodless, his eyes shocked.

"Is he on peyote?" Leaphorn asked. "If he is, they're usually all right after a couple of hours. But if it's not peyote, maybe a doctor should take a look at him."

"It couldn't be peyote," Halsey said, grinning again. "That stuff's illegal, isn't it?"

"It depends," Leaphorn said. "The way the Tribe sees it, it's O.K. if it's used for religious purposes. It's part of the ceremonial of the Native American Church and some of The People belong to that. The way it works, we don't notice people using peyote if they're using it in their religion. I'm guessing Otis here is a religious man."

Halsey caught the irony and **its implications**. His grin became slightly friendly. Otis's eyes were closed now. Susanne was stroking the arch of his right foot. "It's all right now," she was saying. "Oatsy, it's cool." The sympathy in her face confirmed Leaphorn's guess about this young woman. She would tell him all she knew about George Bowlegs for the same reason she now tried to bring Otis back from his **grotesque psychedelic nightmare**.

"Isaacs said the same thing you do," Leaphorn said. "That George wouldn't hurt the Zuñi boy. But that's not the point. It looks like somebody did hurt the Zuñi. Maybe killed him. We think George can tell us something about what happened."

Susanne was now stroking Otis's ankle. Her face was **blank**. "I don't know where he is," she said.

....

its implications what he meant by saying it

grotesque psychedelic nightmare awful nightmare caused by drug use

blank without expression

"I talked to George's little brother today," Leaphorn said. "The boy tells me George is running because he is afraid of something. *Really afraid.* The little brother says George isn't afraid of us, of the police, because he didn't do anything wrong. What's George afraid of?"

Susanne was listening carefully, the stubbornness fading.

"I don't know," Leaphorn continued. "I can't guess. But I can remember being afraid when I was a kid. You ever been really scared? Do you remember how it was?"

"Yes," Susanne said. "I remember."

Like yesterday, Leaphorn thought. Or maybe today. "You get **panicky** and maybe you run," he said. "And if you run it's worse, because you feel like the whole world is chasing you and you're afraid to stop."

"Or there's no place to stop," she said. "Like where would George go to get help? Do you know about his daddy? Being drunk all the time? And most of the time George having to worry about what they're going to eat?"

"Yeah," Leaphorn said. "I've been out there."

"Sometimes there isn't any home to go home to." Susanne seemed to say it to Otis, who wasn't listening.

"The trouble with running out here this time of year is the weather. Today it's late autumn and sunny and no problem. Tomorrow maybe it's winter. Overnight snow and maybe five or six below zero and all of a sudden you don't have any food and no way to get any."

"Does it get that cold here? Below zero?"

....

panicky scared, nervous

"You're almost seven thousand feet above sea level here. Practically sitting on the Continental Divide. Last year it got to fifteen below at Ramah and nineteen below at Gallup. We had eleven **exposure deaths** on the reservation—that we know about."

"But I don't know where he is," she said.

"But just telling me what he said would help me find him," Leaphorn said. "Why did he leave school in the middle of the morning? Why did he come here? What made him run? *Anything* you remember will help. It will help George."

This time Susanne let the silence grow. She might tell me he didn't come here, Leaphorn thought. That was what she had planned. But she wouldn't lie. Not now.

"I don't know exactly," she said. "I know he was afraid of something. He asked if I could give him any food—stuff he could carry that would keep. He wanted to take some of that deer out in the shed. That was George's deer anyway. He brought it to us last week."

"Where was he going?"

"He didn't say."

"But he must have said something. Try to remember everything he said."

"He asked me if I knew anything about the Zuñi religion," Susanne said, "and I said not much. Just a little bit that Ted had told me about it." She paused, **putting the memory back together**. "And then he asked me if Ted had ever told me anything about the kachinas punishing people." She frowned.

....

exposure deaths people die from the cold
putting the memory back together trying to remember

"And if I knew anything about kachina forgiveness."

"Forgiveness?"

"He used the word **'absolution.'** He said, 'If a Zuñi taboo is broken, is there any way to get absolution?' I told him I didn't know anything about it." She looked at Leaphorn curiously. "Is there?"

"I'm not a Zuñi," Leaphorn said. "A Navajo isn't likely to know any more about the Zuñi religion than a white man will know about **Shintoism**."

"It seemed important to George. I could tell that. He kept talking about it."

"Forgiveness for him? Did he give you any idea who needed to be forgiven? Was it him? Or Ernesto?"

"I don't know," Susanne said. "I guessed it was for him, himself. But maybe it was for Ernesto."

"Any hint of what the forgiveness would be for? What sort of . . ." Leaphorn paused, trying for the right word. It wouldn't be crime. Would it be **sacrilege**? He let the sentence dangle and substituted: "Did he say what had happened to offend the kachinas?"

"No. I wondered, too, but it didn't seem the time to ask. He was **all emotional**. In a big hurry. I'd never seen George in a hurry before."

"So he took some venison," Leaphorn said. "How much did he take? And what else?"

Susanne flushed. She tugged the long, grimy sleeve of her sweater down over her knuckles.

'absolution' forgiveness

Shintoism an Asian religion

sacrilege a crime against your religion

all emotional upset

"He didn't take anything," Halsey said. "He asked for it. He didn't get it. I figured he was running from the law, or something, the way he acted. People who live here do not cooperate with a **fugitive**; do not **aid and abet**; do not do a damn thing to give the fuzz any reason to be hassling us." He grinned at Leaphorn. "We **are law-abiding**."

"So he left here without any food," Leaphorn said.

"I made him take my old jacket," Susanne said. She was staring at Halsey, her expression an odd mixture of defiance and fear. "It was an old quilted blue rayon thing with a hole in the elbow."

"What time did he leave?"

"He got here early in the afternoon and I guess he left about ten minutes later—maybe three or three-fifteen."

"And he didn't say anything about where he was going?"

"No," Susanne said. She hesitated. "Not really, anyway. George was kind of a crazy kid. Full of funny ideas. He said he might be gone for a while because he had to find the kachinas."

▷◁

Leaphorn stopped at the fence that sealed the Ramah–Ojo Caliente road off from Navajo allotment grazing lands. He turned off the ignition, yawned. In a moment he would climb from the truck, open the barbed-wire gate, and drive on to Ramah. But now he simply sat, slumped, **surrendering to fatigue**. He had heard of George Bowlegs about noon and

....

fugitive person running from the police
aid and abet help them
are law-abiding follow the law
surrendering to fatigue resting

now it was after midnight. Bowlegs, you little bastard, where are you? Are you sleeping warm? Leaphorn sighed, climbed from the carryall, walked with stiff legs to the gate, opened it, climbed back into the carryall, drove through the gate, climbed out again, shut the gate, climbed back into the truck, and pulled onto the county road in a shower of dust and gravel. He shivered slightly and turned the heater fan higher. Outside the air was absolutely still, the sky cloudless, the moon almost directly overhead. Tonight there would be a hard freeze. And where were George Bowlegs and Ernesto Cata? Dead? Cata perhaps, but it seemed suddenly unlikely. There was no possible reason for anyone to kill him. The blood might have had other sources. Probably this was a wasted day. There was nothing much except the blood. Two square yards of blood stiff earth under a piñion and two boys missing. One of them, everybody said, was a crazy kid. What else was there? Something stolen from an anthropologists' camp—something so **trivial** it hadn't been missed. And something which looked like a Zuñi kachina **snooping** in the moonlight at a hippie commune. What the hell could that have been? He thought again about what his eyes had seen through the binoculars, reshaping the image in his memory. Had his eyes translated something that merely seemed strange under the tricky light into something his imagination suggested? Then what could it have been? A big felt hat oddly creased? No. Leaphorn sighed and yawned. His head was buzzing with his tiredness. He could no longer concentrate. He would sleep at the Ramah chapter house tonight. Tomorrow

---

trivial unimportant
snooping looking around

morning he would check with the Zuñi Police. They would tell him that Cata had come home during the night and confessed to a silly **hoax**. Leaphorn suddenly knew what the explanation would be. A sheep slaughtered for the Shalako feast. The boys saving its blood, using it for an elaborate joke, **unconscious of the cruelty in it**.

Where the road crossed the ridge overlooking the Ramah Valley, Leaphorn slowed, flicked on the radio transmitter. The operator at Ramah would **be long abed**, but Leaphorn raised Window Rock quickly.

There were three messages for him. The captain wanted to know if he was making any progress on the affair of the embezzled payment for the pickup truck. His wife had called to ask that Leaphorn be reminded that he had a dental appointment in Gallup at 2 P.M. And the Zuñi Police Department had called and asked that Leaphorn be informed that Ernesto Cata had been found.

Leaphorn frowned at the radio. "Found? Is that all they said?"

"Let me check," the dispatcher said. "I didn't take the message." The dispatcher sounded sleepy. Leaphorn rubbed his hand across his face, suppressing a yawn.

"Found his body," the dispatcher said.

....

hoax trick; prank

unconscious of the cruelty in it
not realizing it was a cruel joke

be long abed have gone to bed long ago

BEFORE YOU MOVE ON...

1. **Conclusions** Reread pages 61–62. What does Leaphorn think he sees? Why does it scare him?

2. **Character's Motive** Reread page 68. Why is George looking for forgiveness from the kachina?

LOOK AHEAD Read pages 72–89 to learn more about the murderer.

7

Tuesday, December 2, 7:22 A.M.

The sun, rising over Oso Ridge, warmed the right side of Joe Leaphorn's face and cast the shadow of his profile horizontally against the raw gray earth exposed by the landslide. He stood with his arms folded over his stomach, his ears aware of the scraping sound of the shovels but his eyes involved with the beauty of the morning. The view from this **eroded** ridge above Galestina Canyon was impressive. Sunlight struck the east faces of the Zuñi Buttes ten miles to the northwest. It reflected from the yellow water tower that marked the site where the government had built Black Rock to house its Bureau of Indian Affairs people. It flashed now from the wing of a **light plane taking off from** the Black Rock landing strip. Almost due north, three miles up the valley, it **illuminated** the early-morning haze of smoke emerging from the chimneys of Zuñi Village. Much nearer, a yard from the toe of Leaphorn's boot, it lit the scuffed sole of a small, low-cut shoe. The shoe **protruded** from the earth-and-stone rubble of the slide—a black shoe, laces down. It was a track shoe, five spikes under the ball of the foot, none under the heel because a runner's heel

....

eroded worn-down
light plane taking off from small airplane leaving
illuminated brightened; lit up
protruded stuck out

does not strike the ground. Part of the runner's heel was visible, and the Achilles tendon, and perhaps an inch of muscular calf. The earth covered the rest. Leaphorn's gaze rested on Zuñi Village. Halona, they called it. Halona Itawana, the Middle Ant Hill of the World. A hillock beside a bend in the now dry bed of the Zuñi River, a **hillock** of red stone houses jammed together to form the old village and surrounded now by a sprawling cluster of newer houses. Maybe six thousand Zuñis, Leaphorn thought, with something like 6,500 square miles of reservation, and all but a few hundred of them lived like bees in this single busy hive. Up to twenty-five or thirty people in some houses, he had heard. All the daughters of a family still living with their mother, living together with their husbands and their children in a sort of reversal of the Navajos' mother-in-law taboo. It made for the handful of Zuñis a bigger town than the Navajos had made with their 130,000 people. What force caused the Zuñis to **collect** like this? Was it **some polarity** of the force that caused his own Dinee to scatter, to search for loneliness, as much as for grass, wood, and water, as an asset for a hogan site? Was this why the Zuñi had survived as a people against five centuries of **invasions**? Was there some natural law, like the critical mass of nuclear physics, which held that X number of Indians compacted in X number of square yards could resist the White Man's Way by drawing strength from one another?

The plane—silenced by distance—banked toward the north, toward Gallup, or Farmington, or perhaps Shiprock or Chinle, and blinked a quick reflection of sun from a polished surface.

....

hillock little hill
collect live together in one area
some polarity the opposite part
invasions attacks

Just to Leaphorn's left Ed Pasquaanti pushed at the handle of his shovel, hat off, cropped gray hair bristling. Beyond him, three other Zuñis worked methodically. Their last names were Cata, Bacobi, and Atarque. They were the father and uncles, **respectively**, of Ernesto Cata. They dug with deliberate speed, wordlessly. The earth pile **receded**, revealing another inch of Ernesto Cata's calf.

"Where did you find the bicycle?" Leaphorn asked. "If you haven't finished looking there, I could **check around some**." (He had offered once—five minutes ago, when he had first arrived—to help with the digging. "No, thanks," the uncle named Thomas Atarque had said. "We can handle it all right." The earth was Zuñi earth, the body under it Flesh of the Zuñi Flesh. Leaphorn sensed digging here, at this moment in time, was not for a Navajo. He wouldn't repeat the offer.)

"The bike was down there," Pasquaanti said. He pointed. "Pushed under the uphill side of that sandstone outcrop. I just looked around enough to find the tracks leading up this way. It was getting dark then."

The bicycle had been remarkably well hidden considering the circumstances. It had been pushed half under a sandstone overhang and then disguised with a cover of dead grass and weeds. Even with the **camouflage** gone, it was hard to see. Leaphorn looked at it, thinking first that whoever had hidden it had found this site at night. Only moonlight, and two nights ago it would have been a half-moon. The implications of that were clear enough. Whoever had brought Ernesto Cata's body

....

respectively in the order mentioned

receded became smaller

check around some look around the area for awhile

camouflage grass and weeds used to hide it

here to be hidden under a tumbled slide of earth either knew this landscape well or had planned in advance. George Bowlegs would know it and—he thought defensively—a thousand Zuñis would know it. Leaphorn went methodically to work.

The bike had been rolled here up a deer trail. Leaphorn **backtracked** to a sheep path down the slope. The path angled downhill and northward, toward Zuñi Pueblo. He checked everything, working slowly. By the time he reached the cluster of trees where Cata had bled out his life, it was noon. In this small area he spent another three hours—much of it squatted on his heels studying the dusty ground.

There were five sets of recent tracks. He quickly eliminated the Goodyear rubber heel marks left by Pasquaanti and the waffle-soled boots of the Cata uncle who had found the blood. That left cowboy boots, presumably George Bowlegs', which had **dismounted from** the bicycle near the trees, Cata's five-spiked track shoes, and moccasins worn by whoever had pushed the bicycle away with Cata's body as its cargo. Leaphorn sat on a slab of sandstone and considered what these tracks told him. It wasn't much.

He could guess that the killing hadn't been **premeditated**— at least not completely. One who plans to carry a body a long distance uphill over rough ground does not wear moccasins if he has any respect for his feet. He wears something with sturdy sole and heels. The Man Who Wore Moccasins had waited among the junipers out of sight. He could have struck Cata from this **ambush** had there been an intention to kill.

....

backtracked went back over the trail
dismounted from gotten off
premeditated planned
ambush hiding place

But he hadn't. The moccasins had stepped out into the open. Moccasins and track shoes had faced one another long enough for several shuffles and shifts of weight. They had stood very close. (Had Moccasins perhaps gripped Cata's arm?) Then Cata had taken three long stride steps downhill, and fallen, and pumped his blood out onto the thirsty earth. Moccasins now wheeled the bike to the bloody place, loaded Cata upon it, and rolled it away. But it seemed highly unlikely he could have known the bicycle would be available. Not unless Moccasins was George Bowlegs. Could the boy have ridden here in cowboy boots, parked the bike, walked over to the rocks, and changed into moccasins? Obviously, he *could* have. Leaphorn could think of no reasons why he would have. He tried to imagine what Cata and Moccasins might have talked about as they stood toe-to-toe. There was not even **ground for speculation**.

Leaphorn lit a cigarette. A piñon jay emerged from the junipers in a flash of blue feathers and disappeared toward Corn Mountain. A thin blue line of smoke corkscrewed upward from Leaphorn's cigarette to ravel away in the cold air. North, a jet drew a white line across the sky. Behind it the sky was gray **with a high overcast**. Intermittently throughout the dusty autumn, such omens had threatened snow. And all autumn, after a summer **of drought**, the omens had lied. Leaphorn studied the sky, his face **dour**. He was finding no order in his thoughts, none of that mild and abstract pleasure which the precise application of logic always brought to him. Instead

....

ground for speculation a way to guess
with a high overcast and very hazy
of drought without rain
dour unhappy

there was only **the discordant clash of improbable against unlikely, effect without cause, action without motive, patternless chaos**. Leaphorn's orderly mind found this painful. The roughness of the sandstone pressed into his buttocks now, but he ignored this, as he ignored his hunger, willing his thoughts away from these sensations, frowning across the brushy slopes at Corn Mountain, thinking.

Leaphorn came from the Taadii Dinee, the Slow-Talking People Clan. The father of his mother was Nashibitti, a great singer of the Beautyway and the Mountainway, and other curing rites, and a man so wise that it was said the people of Beautiful Mesa added Hosteen to his name when he was less than thirty—calling him Old Man when he was far too young to be a grandfather. Leaphorn had been raised **at the knee of** Hosteen Nashibitti when Nashibitti was old in years as well as wisdom. He had grown up among the sheepmen and hunters of Beautiful Mesa, families who descended from families who had elected to die when Kit Carson's horsemen came in 1864. Thus the handed-down tribal memories which surrounded Leaphorn's boyhood were not, like those of most Navajos of his generation, the grandfather tales of being herded into captivity, of the Long Walk away from the sacred mountains to the concentration camp at Fort Stanton, of smallpox, and the insolent Apaches, and of misery, indignity, and finally the Long Walk home. Instead, the tales of Nashibitti were of the **redder** side of tragedy: of two brothers with bows against a troop of mounted riflemen; of sabered sheep, burning hogans,

....

the discordant clash of improbable against unlikely, effect without cause, action without motive, patternless chaos things that did not make sense

at the knee of by

redder bloodier

the sound of axes cutting down the peach orchards, the bodies of children in the snow, the red of the flames sweeping through the cornfields, and, finally, the **litany** of starving families hunted through the canyons by Kit Carson's **cavalry**. The boy who would become Hosteen Nashibitti and the grandfather of Leaphorn was delivered of a dying mother in such a hungry canyon. He had been raised **with his ears filled with** his uncle's accounts of brutal cruelty and sublime bravery; of how Carson had claimed to be a friend of the Navajos, of how Carson, led by the hated Utes, had ridden through the peaceful cornfields like death on horseback. But somehow, Nashibitti had never learned this bitterness. When he was initiated at the Yeibichai on the last night of the Night Way Ceremonial, the secret war name they gave him had been He Who Asks Questions. But to Leaphorn, seventy years later, he had been One Who Answers. It had been Nashibitti who had taught Leaphorn the words and legends of the Blessing Way, taught him what the Holy People had told the Earth Surface People about how to live, taught him the lessons of the Changing Woman—that the only goal for man was beauty, and that beauty was found only in harmony, and that this harmony of nature was **a matter of dazzling complexity**.

"When the dung beetle moves," Hosteen Nashibitti had told him, "know that something has moved it. And know that its movement affects the flight of the sparrow, and that the raven deflects the eagle from the sky, and that the eagle's stiff wing bends the will of the Wind People, and know that all of

....

litany large number
cavalry soldiers
with his ears filled with listening to
a matter of dazzling complexity beautiful and complicated

this affects you and me, and the flea on the prairie dog and the leaf on the cottonwood." That had always been the point of the lesson. **Interdependency of nature.** Every cause has its effect. Every action its reaction. A reason for everything. In all things a pattern, and in this pattern, the beauty of harmony. Thus one learned to live with evil, by understanding it, by reading its cause. And thus one learned, gradually and methodically, if one was lucky, to always "go in beauty," to always look for the pattern, and to find it.

Leaphorn stabbed the cigarette butt against the rock, grinding it out with an angry gesture. There was no pattern here. Cata was dead without reason. George Bowlegs had not run when he should have run and then he had fled when he shouldn't have. Leaphorn stood and brushed off the seat of his khaki trousers, still thinking. What bothered him most, he realized, were not these large and important **incongruities**. It was smaller ones. Why had Cecil Bowlegs told him that Cata had stolen artifacts from the Early Man dig? There was no reason for Cecil to lie, and no reason for the anthropologists to lie **in denying such a loss**. Why did Cecil think George was running from a vengeful kachina if George had told Susanne he would be *hunting* a kachina? And what was that strange thing Leaphorn had seen at Jason's Fleece with the body of a man and the head of a bird? Could someone be wearing one of the masks of the Zuñi kachina religion? To do so for a purpose outside the religion would surely be the worst sort of sacrilege. There was no possible answer to any of these questions.

....

Interdependency of nature. All things in nature depend on one another.

incongruities things that do not make sense

in denying such a loss about an artifact being stolen

Leaphorn began walking rapidly down the slope toward Zuñi Village. The body would be there by now, the cause of death known. He would find out about that. And when there was time he would learn more about the Zuñi religion. But before he did that, he would get Shorty Bowlegs sober enough to talk—even if he had to **lock him up** to do it.

....

lock him up put him in jail

8

Tuesday, December 2, 6:11 P.M.

The headlights on Joe Leaphorn's Law and Order Division van lost themselves one moment in a blinding gust of reddish-gray dust and the next in the whiteness of a flurry of dry snowflakes. Driving required catching glimpses between gusts and flurries of the twisting, bumpy wagon track and—when it became abruptly invisible—remembering where the wheels would find it. With one tire already blown yesterday on this chancy trail to Shorty Bowlegs' hogan—and no spare left—Leaphorn was taking it very slowly. He was in no particular hurry. He had no real hope that Shorty Bowlegs, if Shorty Bowlegs was sober enough to talk more coherently now, could tell him anything very useful. It was simply that Bowlegs was **the last untapped possibility**. After Bowlegs there would be no place left to go. This was the ultimate **dead end of the Cata affair** and Leaphorn knew himself too well to consider avoiding it. All other possible sources of information had been tapped and the incongruities remained. They would give him no peace. A boy had been killed without reason. Leaphorn's rational mind would not accept this. Not even the grasshopper **took wing** without

....

the last untapped possibility Leaphorn's last chance
dead end of the Cata affair end to the investigation
took wing flew

reason. His mind would worry at the rough edges of this like a tongue at a broken tooth. It would reject Cata killed without cause, George Bowlegs fleeing the scene of this crime a day later than reason said he should have fled the whole irrational business.

Leaphorn turned the carryall down the last slope toward the Bowlegs place. It slid with a bone-jarring thump into a rut. Leaphorn **pronounced an explicit Navajo indecency which took in** darkness, weather, himself, the Zuñi tribe in general, and Ed Pasquaanti in particular. He **swung** the truck across the bare and beaten ground to park.

The headlights lit the Bowlegs brush arbor, flashed for a second on a pole sheep corral down the slope, flicked past the doorway of the Bowlegs hogan and the blue shirted form in its doorway and stopped finally, as Leaphorn set the hand brake, focused on the gray-green foliage of a juniper. Leaphorn turned off the ignition but not the lights. He was relieved. Bowlegs was not only awake, but sober enough to be standing in the doorway, curious about his visitor.

Bowlegs shook out a cigarette, lit it, and waited. Navajo custom and good manners required the wait. The tradition had been born in the old days so that the ghosts which swarmed the reservation and followed travelers would wander impatiently away and not follow the guest into the host's hogan. Today it survived as much out of the respect for privacy of a scattered rural people as from the **waning** threat of the chindi. Without thinking of why he did it, Lieutenant Joe Leaphorn would wait

....

pronounced an explicit Navajo indecency which took in swore in Navajo about

swung drove

waning decreasing, declining

in his truck until Shorty Bowlegs had put on his trousers or otherwise prepared to receive a visitor. And when Bowlegs was ready he would stand outside his hogan door so that Leaphorn would know it.

Leaphorn waited now. The wind shook the truck. It spoke in a dozen voices, whistling, hooting, rasping past cracks and corners and bends of metal. The defroster fan had died with the motor and his breath quickly misted the windshield. Outside spots of white showed where the dusting of dry snow drifted against rocks and eddied into the windbreak of the junipers. The flakes were still tiny, but there were more of them now, wind-driven through the headlight beams. When this **squall line passed**, a real snowstorm might develop. And it was desperately needed. Leaphorn waited, thinking of hungry cattle, dry stock tanks, and the **penalties** of drought; thinking of the long day behind him, of Cata's body on the table at the Black Rock BIA hospital—the doctor cleaning the sand from that great chopped wound which had almost **severed** head from body. An ax, perhaps, or a machete, swung with great force. The funeral had been within the hour. First a funeral Mass at the mission church in the village and then the ceremonial of the Badger kiva at the open grave. He had watched it from a distance, feeling that he was an **intruder into** something sad and private and sacred. Who, he wondered suddenly, would be the Fire God for the Shalako ceremonials now that the Fire God was dead? Leaphorn had no doubt that there would be a new Shulawitsi dancing flawless attendance on the Council

....

squall line passed small storm ended
penalties negative effects
severed separated
intruder into unwanted person at

of the Gods when the ceremonials began. He thought of that, and of where George Bowlegs might be **taking shelter** on this miserable night, and then—abruptly—he was thinking that it was taking far too long for Shorty Bowlegs to reappear at his hogan doorway.

Leaphorn pushed the van door open against the pressure of the wind, pulled his windbreaker collar around his face, and stepped out, staring at the hogan. It was totally dark now. Had it been when he drove up? Leaphorn remembered only his headlights flashing past its entrance, the figure frozen in that flicker of light. He had presumed it was Bowlegs looking out to see who was driving up on this bitter night. But now there was no sign of light around the plank door, none around the small uneven window Bowlegs had cut through the logs of his southeast wall. Would Bowlegs have gone back inside, blown out his kerosene lamp, and left his visitor sitting outside in the cold? Leaphorn thought back, remembering the Bowlegs of yesterday as a friendly man—too drunk to understand what Leaphorn was saying, or for coherent answers, but smiling a wide, wet smile, trying to get Leaphorn to sit, to **join him in a drink**, trying to be helpful.

Leaphorn stood a moment beside the carryall, staring at the dark humped shape of the hogan, aware of the shrieking curses of the wind, of the evil ghosts of a thousand generations of Dinee who rode the night. And then he reached back inside the cab. He fished a flashlight out of the glove compartment and lifted his 30-30 from the rifle rack across the back window. Ten

....

taking shelter staying
join him in a drink have a drink with him

feet from the hogan door he stopped.

"'Ya-ta-hey," he shouted. "Shorty Bowlegs, ya-ta-hey."

The wind whipped a mixture of dust and snow around the hogan, around Leaphorn's feet. The plank door moved, tapping at its crude casement. He stared at the door. In the dim reflection from the headlights he could barely **detect the motion**. He **flicked** on the flashlight. The door was formed of five vertical planks, braced with one-by-four-inch board. Under the yellow light it hung motionless. The wind gusted again, hooting through the hogan's stovepipe smoke hole and speaking in a quarrelsome chorus of voices around the cracks and crevices of its logs. Now the door moved. Outward, then inward, tapping against its latch.

"Hello," Leaphorn shouted. "Shorty?"

The wind voices of the hogan sank abruptly in pitch and volume, answering him with silence. Leaphorn moved beside the hogan wall. He **pumped a shell** into the 30-30 chamber, held the rifle on his right arm. With his left hand he pulled up the doorlatch and jerked outward. The wind helped, sucking the door open and banging it back against the log wall opposite Leaphorn.

Inside nothing moved. The flashlight beam reflected from the **galvanized tin** of a washtub against the back wall, lit a scattered jumble of cooking pots and food supplies, and lingered on clothing (boy-sized bluejeans, three shirts, a nondescript blue cloth, assorted underwear) which hung from the hogan's blanket rope. Behind the clothing, shadows moved

....

detect the motion see the door move
flicked turned
pumped a shell put a bullet
galvanized tin metal

on the rough log wall. Anything there? Nothing visible. Leaphorn moved the light clockwise through the hogan. It passed three empty bedrolls, all **in disarray**, passed a battered metal chest with its drawers hanging open, passed a rope-tied bundle of sheep hides, and stopped finally on the arm of a man. The arm extended limply on the packed earthen floor, the dark wrist thrust out of a sleeve that was khaki (not dark blue), the fingers relaxed, their tips touching the earth.

A stinging flurry of dry snowflakes whipped past Leaphorn's face. Again the wind spoke loud around the hogan, **raising an obbligato mixture of hoots and shrieks**. The flashlight now lit black hair—neatly parted, a braid tied with a string, a cloth headband which had been a faded pink but now was dyed—like the hair beneath it—a fresh bloody **crimson**.

Without knowing it, Leaphorn had been holding his breath. Now that he had found Shorty Bowlegs, he released it with a sound something like a sigh. He stood for a moment looking carefully past the hogan, studying the dim, wind-twisted shapes of the piñons and junipers which surrounded it, examining the shape of the outbuildings. Listening. But the wind made listening useless.

He stepped into the hogan and squatted on his heels. He stared first at the face that had been Bowlegs' and then examined the hogan. Shorty Bowlegs had been killed with a blow struck from behind with something heavy and sharp. The same weapon that had killed Cata? Swung by the figure in the blue shirt (a man, he thought, without knowing why he thought

....

in disarray messy
raising an obbligato mixture of hoots and shrieks making strange noises
crimson red

it) he had seen at the doorway. And where was that man now? Not more than five minutes away, but with wind, snow, dust, and darkness making both ears and eyes useless, he might as well be on another planet. Leaphorn cursed himself. He had seen this killer, and he had sat daydreaming in his truck while the man walked away.

Leaphorn **tested** the blood on Bowlegs' hair with a tentative fingertip. Sticky. Bowlegs had been struck at least thirty minutes before Leaphorn's arrival. The killer had apparently killed Bowlegs first and then **ransacked** the hogan. Had he come to kill Bowlegs and, with that done, searched the family's belongings? Or had he come to make the search and killed Bowlegs to make it possible? To search for what? Everything that Bowlegs had **accumulated** in perhaps forty years of living was **littered** on the hogan floor. Add it together—the clothing, the supplies, the sheepherder's tools—and it might have cost five hundred dollars, new, at inflated trading post prices. Now it was worn, used. By whiteman's standards, Leaphorn thought, Bowlegs had a net worth of maybe one hundred dollars. The white world's measure of his life. And what would the Navajo measure be? The Dinee made a harder demand—that man find his place in the harmony of things. There, too, Shorty Bowlegs had failed.

Outside the hogan, Leaphorn snapped off the carryall headlights and began a search in gradually widening circles. He worked slowly, conscious that the killer—unlikely as it seemed—might still be near. He looked for tracks—human,

....

tested touched
ransacked searched
accumulated collected and saved
littered lying

horse, or vehicle—using his flashlight sparingly in places where they might be preserved from the wind. He found **nothing very conclusive**. His own van's tires showed up in several places where the gusts had not erased them, but no other vehicle had apparently come near the hogan recently. Having established that, he **made a careful inspection of the pen in a shallow arroyo** below the hogans which had served as the Bowlegs stables. Two horses had been kept there. The tracks of one—poorly shod—were only a few hours old. The other had apparently not been around for perhaps a day. Leaphorn squatted on the loamy earth, hunched against the icy wind, thinking about what that might mean.

The wind rose and fell, now whipping the limbs of the junipers into frantic thrashing, now dying into an almost silent lull. Leaphorn snapped off the light and crouched motionless. The wind had carried an **incongruous** sound. He listened. It was buried now under the thousand sounds of the storm. And then he heard it again. A bell. And then another, slightly lower in pitch. And a third with a tinny tinkle. Leaphorn moved swiftly toward a gnarled juniper barely visible in the darkness, toward the sound. He stood behind the tree, waiting. The bells approached, and with them the sound of a horse. The dim shape of a white goat tinkled past the tree, followed by a straggling stream of goats and then an almost solid mass of

....

nothing very conclusive no evidence

made a careful inspection of the pen in a shallow arroyo carefully searched a fenced area in a ditch

incongruous odd

sheep. Finally, there came the horse, and on it a small shape, huddled against the cold.

Leaphorn stepped from behind the **juniper**.

"Ya-ta-hey," he shouted. "Cecil?"

....

juniper tree

BEFORE YOU MOVE ON...

1. **Summarize** Reread pages 74–76. Cata's body is found. What does Leaphorn learn about the killer?

2. **Plot** Reread pages 86–87. Who is the man in Shorty Bowleg's doorway? What mistake does Leaphorn make?

LOOK AHEAD Read pages 90–103 to find out why the FBI becomes involved in the case.

9

Tuesday, December 2, 10:15 P.M.

It was almost two hours later when Leaphorn reached Zuñi and left Cecil with a young Franciscan brother at Saint Anthony's school. He had told Cecil as gently as he could that someone had struck his father on the back of the head and that Shorty Bowlegs was dead. He had radioed New Mexico State Police at Gallup to **make this homicide a matter of record** and the dispatcher had promised to notify Zuñi Police and the McKinley County sheriff's office. That would assure that the routine would be properly followed, although Leaphorn was sure that whoever had killed Shorty Bowlegs would not be stupid enough to be captured at a **roadblock**. With these official duties done, Leaphorn had helped Cecil unsaddle the horse and secure the sheep in the brush corral. He had left Cecil in the cab of the truck then, with the motor running and the heater on high, while he recovered the boy's bedroll and odds and ends of spare clothing from the hogan. He put these—a single shirt, three pairs of cheap socks, and underwear—in an empty grocery sack. He **handed** the sack through the truck window.

---

make this homicide a matter of record officially report this murder
roadblock place on the road where police stop cars
handed gave Cecil

"I didn't find any pants."

"Just got these I got on," Cecil said.

"Anything else you want out of there?"

Cecil stared over his shoulder at the hogan. Leaphorn wondered what he was thinking. Two hours ago when he had left to bring in the sheep that humped shape had been home. Warm. Occupied by a man who, drunk or not, was his father. Now the hogan was cold, hostile to him, occupied not by Shorty Bowlegs but by Shorty's ghost—a ghost which would **in Navajo fashion embody** only those things in his father's nature which were weak, evil, angry.

"Ought to get George's stuff out of there, I guess," Cecil said. He paused. "What do you think—would they have ghost sickness on them yet? And I've got a lunchbox. You think we should leave that stuff?"

"I'll get 'em. And tomorrow we'll get somebody to come out here and **take care of** the body and **fix up** the hogan. There won't be any ghost sickness."

"Just the lunchbox for me," Cecil said. "That's all I got."

It occurred to Leaphorn, back inside the hogan, that this would be an unusually complicated death. No relatives around to arrange for disposal of the body, and to break a hole through a hogan wall to release Shorty's ghost for its infinite wandering, and to nail shut the door as a warning to all that here stood a hogan **contaminated** by death, and—finally—to find the proper Singer, and arrange the proper Sing, to cure any of those who might have been somehow touched and endangered

....

in Navajo fashion embody represent like a Navajo

take care of remove

fix up remove spirits from

contaminated polluted; made dirty

by this death. More important, there was no surrounding family to **absorb the survivors**—to engulf a child with the love of uncles and aunts and cousins, to give Cecil the security of a new hogan and a new family. The family to do this must be somewhere on the Ramah reservation. It would be part of Shorty's family. Since Cecil's mother was no good, it would be better to return him to the outfit of his father's mother. The people at the Ramah chapter house would know where to find them. And for Leaphorn there then remained the matter of finding Cecil's big brother.

In the hogan, he found surprisingly little trace of George. A spare shirt, too ragged even for George to wear, and a few odds and ends similarly rejected. Nothing else. Leaphorn added this lack of George's belongings to the absence of the second Bowlegs horse from the corral and came to the obvious conclusion. George had come back to this hogan the day that horse had left its latest tracks at the corral. That was yesterday, the day after Cata had died. George had picked up his spare clothing and the horse. He must have been here not long after Leaphorn had made his **fruitless first call on Shorty**.

On his way out of the hogan, Leaphorn saw what must be Cecil's lunchbox. **It was one of those tin affairs sold in the dime stores.** Its yellow paint was decorated with a picture of Snoopy atop his doghouse. It lay open now beside the hogan wall. Leaphorn picked it up.

Inside the box were a dozen or so papers, once neatly folded but now pawed through and left in disarray. The top one was

....

absorb the survivors take care of Cecil

fruitless first call on Shorty first visit to Shorty

It was one of those tin affairs sold in dimes stores. It was a cheap lunchbox.

filled with penciled subtraction problems and bore the notation "GOOD!" in red ink. The paper under it was titled "Paragraphs" in the upper left corner. Above the title a gold star was pasted.

Leaphorn refolded the papers. Under them were a small blue ball with a broken bit of rubber band attached, a spark plug, a small horseshoe magnet, a ball of copper wire wound neatly on a stick, an aspirin bottle half filled with what looked like dirty iron filings, the wheel off a toy car, and a stone figure a little larger than Leaphorn's thumb. It was the **elongated** shape of a mole carved from a piece of antler. Two thin buckskin thongs secured a tiny chipped flint arrowhead to its top. It was obviously a fetish figure, probably from one of the Zuñi medicine fraternities. It certainly wasn't Navajo.

In the van, Cecil was looking through the windshield. He took the box without a word and put it on his lap. They jolted past the hogan with Cecil still staring straight ahead.

"I'm going to leave you at Saint Anthony's Mission tonight," Leaphorn said. "Then I'm going to find George and get both of you boys away from here. I'm going to get you to your father's family unless you feel there's somewhere else that would be better."

"No," Cecil said. "There's no place else."

"Where'd you get that fetish?"

"Fetish?"

"That little bone mole."

"George gave it to me."

"What does your other horse look like?"

----

elongated long

"The other horse? It's a bay. Big, with white stockings."

"When George came and got the horse, what else did he take?"

Cecil said nothing. His hands gripped the lunchbox. Between the boy's fingers Leaphorn could **make out the inscription**: "Happiness is a strong kite string."

"Look," Leaphorn said. "If he didn't take the horse, who did? And who took his things? Don't you think we should find him now? Don't you think he'd be safer? For God's sake, think about it for a minute."

The carryall tilted up the slope above the hogan, grinding in second gear. A fresh **assault** of wind howled past its windows. The snow had stopped now and the vehicle was **submerged in** a sea of swirling dust. Cecil suddenly began shaking. Leaphorn put his hand on the boy's shoulder. He was overcome with a wild **surge** of anger.

"He got the horse yesterday evening," Cecil said. His voice was very small. "It was about dark, after I talked to you. My father, he was asleep, and I went out to see about the sheep and when I got back the rifle was gone and I found the note." Cecil was still staring straight ahead, his hands gripping the tin box so hard that his knuckles whitened. "And I guess he took his knife, and the stuff he kept in a leather pouch he made, and a part of a loaf of bread." Cecil fell silent, the catalog completed.

"Where'd he say he was going?"

"The note's in here with my stuff," Cecil said. He unlatched the box and sorted through the papers. "I thought I put it in

....

make out the inscription read the writing

assault gust

submerged in inside

surge feeling

here," he said. He shut the box. "Anyway, I remember most of it. He said he couldn't explain it to me exactly, but he was going to find some kachinas. He said he had to talk to them. He couldn't pronounce the name of the place. He tried to say it, but all I remember was it started with a 'K.' And when he **was riding off** he said he'd be gone several days to where this kachina was, **taking care of the business he had**. And if he couldn't get it done there, then he'd have to go to Shalako over at Zuñi and then he'd be home. And he said not to worry about him."

"Did he say anything about Ernesto Cata?"

"No."

"Or give any hint where he was looking for this kachina?"

"No."

"Was that all he said?"

Cecil didn't answer. Leaphorn glanced at him. The boy's eyes were wet.

"No," Cecil said. "He said to take care of Dad."

....

was riding off left on his horse

taking care of the business he had doing what he needed to do

>> **10** <<

Wednesday, December 3, 10 A.M.

Joe Leaphorn was having trouble concentrating. It seemed to him that a single homicide (as the death of Cata) could be thought of as a unit—as something in which an act of violence contained beginning and end, cause and result. But two homicides linked by time, place, participants, and, most important, **motivation** presented something more complex. The unit became a sequence, the dot became a line, and lines tended to extend, to lead places, to move in directions. One-two became one-two-three-four. . . . Unless, of course, the deaths of the Zuñi boy and the drunken Navajo **were the sum of some totality**. Could this be?

This question was the focus of Leaphorn's concentration. Did the killing of Cata and of Shorty Bowlegs make sense in themselves? Or must they be part of something larger? And if **the sequence was incomplete**, where did the line between Cata and Bowlegs point? The question cried for every gram of Leaphorn's attention. His head ached with it.

But there were distractions. The FBI agent was talking. Once again a fly was patrolling the Zuñi Police Department

---

motivation the reason for killing

were the sum of some totality were the only people the murderer intended to kill

the sequence was incomplete there were to be more murders

96

office. And outside a truck whined down the asphalt of N.M. 53 with something noisily wrong with its gearbox. Leaphorn found himself thinking of the late Ernesto Cata, who had (as the Zuñis would say it) **completed his path after thirteen years of life**, who had been the personifier of the Fire God, an altar boy at Saint Anthony's Church, a baptized Christian, a Catholic communicant, a member of a Zuñi kiva fraternity born into the Badger Clan, who would almost certainly have become one of the "valuable men" of the Zuñi religion had not someone, for some reason, found it expedient to kill him.

The voice of Agent John O'Malley intruded itself on Leaphorn's consciousness. He raised his eyebrows at the FBI man to **simulate attention**.

". . . ask enough people," O'Malley was saying. "We tend to find that someone finally remembers seeing something helpful. It's a matter of patiently . . ."

Leaphorn found his attention diverted again. Why, he was thinking, were FBI agents so often exactly like O'Malley? He saw that the white man who sat behind O'Malley had noticed the eyebrow gesture, had interpreted it for exactly what it was, and was grinning at Leaphorn a friendly, sympathetic, lopsided grin. This man was maybe fifty, with a pink, freckled, sagging, hound-dog face and a shock of sandy hair. O'Malley had introduced him simply as "Agent Baker." As O'Malley must have intended, this **left the impression** that Baker was another FBI agent. It had occurred to Leaphorn earlier that Baker was not, in fact, an agent of the Federal Bureau of Investigation. He

....

completed his path after thirteen years of life died at the age of thirteen

simulate attention pretend he was listening

left the impression made others think

didn't look like one. He had bad teeth, irregular and discolored, and an air of casual sloppiness, and something about him which suggested a quick, inquisitive, impatient intelligence. Leaphorn's extensive experience with the FBI suggested that any of these three characteristics would prevent employment. The FBI people always seemed to be O'Malleys—trimmed, scrubbed, tidy, **able to work untroubled by any special measure of intelligence**. O'Malley was still talking. Leaphorn looked at him, wondering about this FBI policy. Where *did* they find so many O'Malleys? He had a sudden vision of an office in the Department of Justice building in Washington, a clerk sending out draft notices to all the male cheerleaders and drum majors at U.S.C., Brigham Young, Arizona State, and Notre Dame, ordering them to get their hair cut and report for duty. He suppressed a grin. Then it occurred to him that he had seen Baker before. It had been in Utah, in the office of the San Juan County sheriff, in the wake of an **autopsy** which showed that a Navajo rodeo performer had died of an overdose of heroin. Baker had been there, looking sloppy and amused, offering the sheriff credentials from the Narcotics Control Division of the Justice Department's Bureau of Narcotics and Dangerous Drugs. That had been a long time ago. It had been followed by reports of arrests made in Flagstaff, and by a variety of vaguish rumors of the sort which circulate among **the brethren of the law**, rumors suggesting that Mr. Baker had **pulled quite a coup**, that he was smarter than one should expect and apparently more ruthless as well.

....

able to work untroubled by any special measure of intelligence not very smart

autopsy examination of a dead body

the brethren of the law police officers

pulled quite a coup tricked everyone

So Baker is a **narc**. Leaphorn's mind instantly sought the proper place and perspective for this new bit of information. A narcotics agent was involving himself in the deaths of Ernesto Cata and Shorty Bowlegs. Why? And why had O'Malley tried to conceal this fact from local officers? On the surface both answers were obvious. Baker was here because some federal authority somewhere suspected illicit drugs were involved in this affair. And O'Malley hadn't introduced Baker properly because he didn't want the Navajo Police, or the Zuñi Police, or the New Mexico State Police, or the McKinley County Sheriff's Office, to know a narc was at work here. But the answers raised new questions. What had aroused this federal suspicion of drugs? And who had **cut the locals out of the picture**? Which agency did they think would be leaking?

Leaphorn examined the FBI agent. ". . . if there's any physical evidence which leads us anywhere we'll find it," O'Malley was saying. "There's always something. Some little thing. But you people know this part of the country better than we do—and you know the local people . . ." O'Malley was a handsome man, square-jawed, long faced, the unhealthy whiteman pallor tanned away, the light hair sunburned lighter, the mouth a quick affair of lips and cheek muscles and white teeth. Was he **green** enough to believe that none of the men in the room would know that Baker was a narc? Or was he arrogant enough not to care if they detected the insult?

Leaphorn glanced at Pasquaanti, who was gazing at O'Malley with **placid and inscrutable** interest. The Zuñi's

....

narc narcotics officer; policeman who fights drug crimes
cut the locals out of the picture decided not to tell local police
green inexperienced, new
placid and inscrutable calm and mysterious

face told Leaphorn nothing. Highsmith was slumped in his chair, fiddling with his state police uniform cap, his legs stretched in front of him and his eyes invisible to Leaphorn. Orange Naranjo's stern old face was turned toward the window, his black eyes bored and restless. Leaphorn watched him. Saw him briefly turn to examine Baker, watch O'Malley, glance back toward the window. Some vague hint of anger among the wrinkles suggested to Leaphorn that Naranjo, too, remembered who Baker was. Naranjo's job, as assigned by O'Malley, was to cover the non-Navajo **periphery** of the Zuñi reservation, talking to ranchers, road crews, telephone linemen, anyone who might have noticed anything. Leaphorn wondered how hard he would work at it. "We would be interested if someone had seen any strangers, anything unusual, maybe a light plane flying low, maybe who knows what . . ."

"Yeah," Naranjo said.

"Country this empty, people notice strangers," O'Malley said. Leaphorn had glanced quickly at Naranjo, curious about how he would react to this **inanity**.

"Yeah," Naranjo had said, looking slightly surprised.

O'Malley now looked at Leaphorn. It had been made clear earlier that the agent was not happy with Lieutenant Leaphorn. Leaphorn should not have **prowled** around in the Bowlegs hogan after he had found the Bowlegs body. He shouldn't have returned to the hogan at daylight this morning in his fruitless hunt for any tire tracks, footprints, or fragments that the wind might have left. Leaphorn should have backed carefully away

....

periphery outer edges
inanity ridiculous comment
prowled searched

and not interfered with the work of the experts. None of this had been said, but it had been **implied** in the questions with which O'Malley had interrupted Leaphorn's terse account of what had happened at the Bowlegs hogan.

"Baker and I'll head out to the Bowlegs place now," O'Malley said, "and see if there's any prints, or anything for the lab to work on. It would be helpful, Lieutenant, if you'd check among your people living around here and see what you can **pick up**. Sort of like Naranjo's going to do. O.K.?"

"O.K.," Leaphorn said.

O'Malley paused at the door. "We'd sure like to talk to George Bowlegs," he said to Leaphorn.

The silence Baker and O'Malley left behind them lasted maybe ten seconds. Highsmith rose, stretched, and adjusted his visored cap.

"Well, shee-it," he said. "Time to **put the tired body back behind the wheel and run errands for the Effy-Bee-Eye**." He grinned down at Naranjo. "Country as empty as this, people notice strangers. Bet that never occurred to you before, Orange?"

Naranjo made a wry face. "Oh, well," he said. "He's probably all right when you get to know him."

Highsmith reached for the doorknob, then paused. "Any you birds know anything that makes it look like narcotics is mixed up in this?"

Leaphorn laughed.

"You mean besides Baker being a Treasury man?"

....

implied suggested

pick up find out

put the tired body back behind the wheel and run errands for the Effy-Bee-Eye get back in the car and run errands for the FBI

Naranjo asked.

"I was wondering about Baker," Pasquaanti said. "He didn't look like FBI." He paused. "And now I'm wondering why O'Malley didn't tell us who he was."

"They found out about that **treaty** you Zuñis made with the Turks to become the **global center** of opium production," Highsmith said. "They don't want the Zuñi Police Department to know they're investigating."

"It's like my daddy always told me," Pasquaanti said. "Never trust no goddamn **Induns**. That right, Lieutenant?"

"That's right," Leaphorn said. "My grandmother had a motto hanging there in the hogan when I was a kid. Said 'Beware All Blanket-Asses.' "

Naranjo put on his hat, which, despite the season, was straw. "Somebody should have warned Custer," he said.

Highsmith was out the door now. "That motto," he shouted back at Leaphorn. "How did she spell Blanket-Ass in Navajo?"

"Capital B," Leaphorn said.

Outside the sun beat down from a dark blue sky. The air was still and cold and very dry.

"The weather's decided to **behave itself**," Highsmith said. "Last night I thought winter was finally going to get here."

"I don't like these late winters," Naranjo said. "Too damn dry and then when it does come, it's usually a son of a bitch."

Pasquaanti was leaning on the doorsill. Naranjo climbed into his car. "Well," he said, "I guess I'll go chasing around seeing if I can find . . ." The rest of it was drowned by the roar

....

treaty agreement
global center world leader
Induns Indians; Native Americans

of Highsmith's engine as the state policeman made a backing turn and then **shot away** down New Mexico Highway 53.

Leaphorn put his carryall into gear and followed. He turned eastward, toward the intersection with the Ojo Caliente road, toward the commune which called itself Jason's Fleece. He had told O'Malley and Pasquaanti about the note George Bowlegs left for Cecil. O'Malley hadn't been interested. Pasquaanti had looked thoughtful, and finally had shaken his head and said that he'd heard Bowlegs was kind of a crazy kid, but offered no hint of explanation. Leaphorn decided he would tell Susanne of the note, and then talk to Isaacs about it, hoping for some forgotten **crumb** of information which might **point in the direction Bowlegs had taken**. The knobby rubber of his mud tires produced a spray of gravel on the county road and then a rooster tail of dust as he jolted down the wagon track toward the commune. He was thinking that while Bowlegs was hunting his kachina, something was almost certainly hunting Bowlegs. Joe Leaphorn, who almost never hurried, was hurrying now.

....

behave itself stay warm and sunny

shot away drove quickly

crumb piece

point in the direction Bowlegs had taken lead Leaphorn to Bowlegs

BEFORE YOU MOVE ON...

1. **Character's Point of View** Reread pages 98–99. Why is Leaphorn suspicious of Baker and why he is there?

2. **Paraphrase** What does O'Malley mean when he says "Country this empty, people notice strangers"?

LOOK AHEAD Read pages 104–119 to find out what Susanne knows about the disappearances.

≫ **11** ≪

Wednesday, December 3, 12:15 P.M.

A young man with peeling sunburn and blond hair tied in a
bun was working with a portable welding torch in the commune
school bus. The noise it was making had covered the sound
of Leaphorn's carryall rolling to a stop and he was obviously
startled when he saw the policeman.

"She's busy," he told Leaphorn. "I don't think she's around
here. What kind of business do you have with her?"

"Private kind," Leaphorn said mildly. "That is, unless
you're a friend of George Bowlegs. We're trying to find where
the Bowlegs boy **got off to**." Behind Hair in Bun, the blanket
covering the door of the hogan of Alice Madman's ghost
moved. A face appeared, stared at Leaphorn, disappeared. A
second later, Halsey pushed past the blanket and **emerged**.

"You're a cop," Hair in Bun said.

"Like it says there," Leaphorn said, waving in the direction
of the Navajo Police seal on the carryall door, "I'm Navajo
fuzz." Halsey's expression had amused him and he repeated it
loudly enough for Halsey to hear.

"Ya-ta-hey," Halsey said. "Sorry, but that kid you're hunting

....

got off to went
emerged came outside

104

ain't been back."

"Well, then," Leaphorn said, "I'll just talk to Susanne a little more and see if she's remembered anything that might help."

"She hasn't," Halsey said. "We'll **get word to you if anything comes up**. No use you wasting your time."

"Don't mind," Leaphorn said. "It **beats** working. What you fixing on that bus?" The question was addressed to Hair in Bun. The man stared at him.

"Loose seat," Halsey said.

"Be damned," Leaphorn said. "You're welding it back instead of bolting it down? Like to see how you're doing that." He moved toward the bus door.

Hair in Bun stepped into the doorway, pulled his hands out of the bib of his overalls, and let them hang by his sides. Leaphorn stopped.

"**I've got a one-track mind**," he told Halsey. "The only thing I want to do is talk to Susanne and see if we can figure out a way to find that boy. But if Susanne is off somewhere, I'll **kill some time by** looking around some." He looked at Hair in Bun. "Starting with this bus," he said. The voice remained mild.

"I think she's over by the windmill," Halsey said. "I'll take you over there."

The path wandered maybe 150 yards down into a narrow wash and then up its sand-and-gravel bottom toward the wall of the mesa from which Leaphorn had watched the commune two nights earlier. Just under the mesa, an intermittent seep had produced a marshy spot. Some grazing leaser had drilled

....

get word to you if anything comes up tell you if he comes
beats is better than
I've got a one-track mind I only want one thing

a shallow well, installed a windmill to pump a trickle of water into a sheep watering tank. A Russian olive beside the tank was **festooned** with drying shirts, jeans, overalls, and underwear. Susanne was sitting in its shade, watching them approach.

"Did you find him? Did George come home?"

"No. I was hoping we could **go over it all** again and maybe you'd remember something that would help."

"I don't think there's anything to remember." She shook her head. "I just don't think he told me anything except what I could remember Monday."

"Like I told you," Halsey said.

Leaphorn ignored him. "You said George asked you if you knew anything about the Zuñi religion," Leaphorn said. "Can you remember anything more about that part of the conversation?"

Behind him, Halsey laughed.

"Really. Really, I can't." She was looking past him at Halsey. "I just remember he asked me if I knew anything and I told him just what little Ted had told me about it. I'd help if I could."

"O.K.," Halsey said. "Come on, Navajo policeman, let's go."

Leaphorn turned. Halsey was standing in the path, hands in the pockets of the army **fatigue** jacket he was wearing, looking amused and **insolent**. He was a big man, tall and heavy in the shoulders. Leaphorn let his anger show in his voice.

"I'm just saying this once. This girl and I are going to talk awhile without you interrupting. We can talk here, or we can talk in the sheriff's office in Gallup. And if we go to Gallup,

....

kill some time by spend my time
festooned covered
go over it all talk about it
fatigue uniform

you and that **illegal deer carcass** will go along. Possession of an untagged mule deer carcass **out of season** will cost you maybe three hundred dollars and a little time in jail. And then you're going to go to Window Rock and talk to the Tribe's people about what the hell you're doing on Navajo land without a permit."

"It's public domain land," Halsey said. "It's off the reservation. Bureau of Land Management land."

"Our map shows it's on the **res**," Leaphorn said. "But you can argue with the magistrate about that. After you **get clear of** the sheriff at Gallup."

"O.K.," Halsey said. He looked past Leaphorn at Susanne—a long, baleful stare—turned on his heel, and walked rapidly down the draw toward the commune.

"But I still don't remember anything," Susanne said. She was looking after Halsey, her lower lip caught in her teeth.

Leaphorn leaned his hips against the steep arroyo bank behind him and watched Halsey out of sight. "How could anybody possibly find him?" Susanne added. "Either he ran away for good or pretty soon he'll come home. There's no use chasing him. I've been thinking about what you told me about the cold weather." She looked at him defiantly. "I don't think I really believe George will freeze. If the foxes and coyotes and things like that don't freeze, I bet George wouldn't. He's just as at home out there as they are. What you were telling me was just crap, wasn't it? Just something to get me to talk about him?"

....

insolent rude, disrespectful
illegal deer carcass deer that was killed illegally
out of season when it is not hunting season
res reservation

"I wanted you to talk about him, yes," Leaphorn said. "And from what I hear, George is smart and tough. But we did have those eleven people freeze last winter. Some of them were old, and one was sick, and one had been thrown by his horse, but some of them were mature, healthy men. Just too much snow, too cold, too far from shelter."

"I'll bet they were drunk," Susanne said.

Leaphorn laughed. "O.K. If you made a bet like that, I guess you'd win. Three of them were drunk. I wouldn't worry much about George if he had plenty of food. If he isn't hungry, and a snowstorm **catches him**, he can keep a fire going."

"He'll get food," Susanne said. "He killed that deer for us, you know. And he must be just about the greatest deer hunter. He's been keeping his family supplied with meat since he was just a little boy. And he knows everything about deer."

"Like what?"

"Like . . . I don't know. What was it he was telling me?" She made a nervous gesture with her hands, recalling it. "Like deer have their eyes so far on the sides of their heads they can see a lot better behind them than we can. They can see except almost directly behind them. But then he said that deer **are mostly color blind** and . . . what was it he said? . . . they don't recognize shapes very well to the sides of them because they don't have stereoscopic vision as good as we do. Anyway, he said they see things like motion and flashes of reflections better than us . . . but it's mostly **two dimensional**. He told me that one day he was standing real still in plain view with two mule

---

get clear of are allowed to leave

catches him comes

are mostly color blind cannot see color

two dimensional flat

deer about seventy-five yards away staring at him. And just to test them, he opened his mouth. Didn't make any noise or anything. Just opened his mouth. And both deer ran away."

"**They're very far-sighted**," Leaphorn said.

"So I think, if he gets hungry, he'll kill a deer," she said.

"With what?"

"Didn't he stop and get his daddy's rifle?"

"Did he say he would?"

Susanne's expression said she hadn't meant to tell him that. "I guess maybe he did," she said slowly. "Or maybe I just presumed he would."

"Did he tell you anything else about deer hunting?"

"Lots of things. He was teaching Ernesto how to hunt, and Ernesto was teaching him the Zuñi way of hunting. I think he was, whatever that is. Anyway, they talked about hunting a lot." She **made a wry face**. "Frankly, I learned more about it than I need to know."

"Like what else?" Leaphorn asked. "If Bowlegs was **living off the land**, knowing how much he knew about hunting deer could be useful."

"Like deer don't look up. So if you can get up on a cliff or something above them they won't see you." She stuck up a second finger. "Like they have a great sense of smell." A third finger went up. "And a great sense of hearing." She laughed. "So if you're up on that boulder, they won't see you but they smell you and hear you breathing. But they don't smell so well in extremely dry weather, and hardly anything if it's raining

---

They're very far-sighted They can see things far away

made a wry face looked disgusted

living off the land surviving by eating things in nature

or heavy fog, or if the wind is blowing hard. But for miles if there's normal humidity and just a breeze." A fourth finger went up. "And like they don't notice natural sounds much, so if you're moving you're supposed to move right down the deer trail where they'd expect to hear noise, and you move in a sort of stop-and-go pace"—she made **vaguish** hand motions—"like the deer do themselves if there's a lot of leaves and stuff." She stopped, remembering, frowning. "George said the only noise that scares them is something strange, the wrong kind of noise or coming from the wrong place."

She looks tired and thin, Leaphorn was thinking. What the hell is she doing here with this **hard bunch**? She's too young. Why don't white people take care of their children? Then he thought of George Bowlegs. And why don't Navajos take care of their children?

"You said Ernesto was teaching him the Zuñi way to hunt," Leaphorn said. "What was that?"

"Maybe they were just joking," she said. "I guess it was religion, though. There was a poem, a little song. You're supposed to sing it when you **go after** mule deer. George was trying to memorize it in Zuñi, and it was hard because he is just beginning to speak Zuñi. I had them translate it and I wrote it down in my notebook."

"I'd like to see it," Leaphorn said. He would like very much to see the notebook, he thought. And so would Baker. What else had she **jotted down** in it?

"I can just about remember part of it." She paused.

....

vaguish slight
hard bunch tough group of people
go after hunt

"Deer, Deer, Strong Male Deer,
I am the sound you hear running in your hoofprints,
I following come, the sound of running.
Sacred favors for you I bring.
My arrow carries new life for you."

Her voice, small and **fluting**, stopped abruptly. She glanced sidewise at Leaphorn, flushed. "There's a lot more of it, I think, and I probably got it wrong. And then there's a prayer when the deer falls. You take his muzzle in your hands and you put your face against his nostrils and you inhale his breath, and you say, 'Thank you, my father. This day I have drunken in the sacred wind of your life.' I think that's beautiful," she said. "I think the Zuñis have a beautiful . . ." Her voice **trailed off**. She put her head down, her hands over her face. "Ernesto was so happy," she said, the voice muffled by her hands. "Happy people shouldn't have to die."

"I don't know," Leaphorn said. "Maybe death should only be for the very old. The people who are tired and want some rest." Susanne wasn't making any sound. She sat with her head down, her face in her hands. Leaphorn talked about it quietly. He told her how the Navajo mythology dealt with it, how Monster Slayer and Child Born of Water took the weapons they had stolen from the Sun and how they killed the Monsters who brought death to the Dinee, but how they decided to **spare** one kind of death. "We call it Sa," Leaphorn said. "The way my grandfather told me the story, the Hero Twins found Sa

....

jotted down written
fluting pretty
trailed off became quieter and then was silent
spare not kill; save

sleeping in a hole in the ground. Born of Water was going to kill him with his club, but Sa woke up, and he told the twins that they should spare him so that those who are worn out and tired with age can die to make room for others being born."

He intended to keep talking just as long as she needed him to talk so that she could cry without embarrassment. She wasn't crying for Ernesto Cata, really, but for herself, and for George Bowlegs, and all the lost children, and all the lost innocence. And now she was wiping her face with the back of her hand, and now with the sleeve of her overlarge shirt.

How old is she? Leaphorn wondered. In her late teens, probably. But her age seemed crazily mixed. As green as spring, as gray as winter. How had she come here? Where had she come from? Why didn't the white man take care of his daughter? Was he, like Shorty Bowlegs, hiding from his children **in a bottle**?

"I hope all that about hunting helps, but I don't see how it could," she said. "I think you should wait for him to come home again."

"I haven't told you about that," Leaphorn said. "There's isn't any home for George anymore. You knew his dad was an alcoholic, I guess. Well, now his dad is dead."

"My God!" Susanne said. "Poor George. He doesn't know yet?"

"Not unless—" Leaphorn checked himself. "No," he said. "He hasn't been back."

"He was ashamed of his dad," Susanne said. "Ashamed of

----

in a bottle by drinking too much

him being drunk all the time. But he liked him, too. You could tell that. He really loved him."

"So did Cecil," Leaphorn said.

"It's different when they're drunks, I think," Susanne said. "That's like your father being sick. He can't really help it. You can still love them then and it's not so bad." She paused. Her eyes were wet again, but she ignored it. "Now he doesn't have anything. First he loses Ernesto and now he loses his dad."

"He has a brother," Leaphorn said. "An eleven-year-old brother named Cecil. He's got Cecil, but until we can find George, Cecil doesn't have him."

"I didn't know he had a brother," Susanne said. "Not until you **mentioned it**. He never said anything about him." She said it as if she found it incredible, as if she suddenly didn't quite understand George Bowlegs. She stood up, put her hands in the pockets of her jeans, nervously took them out again. They were small hands, frail, grimy, with broken nails. "I have a sister," she said. "**Fourteen** in January. Someday, I'm going back and get her." Susanne was looking **down the wash**. "When I have some money someday I'll go back and go to the school at lunch hour and I'll take her away with me."

"And bring her here?"

Susanne looked at him. "No. Not bring her here. Find someplace to take her."

"Isn't she better off with your parents?"

"Parent," Susanne corrected **absently**. "No. I don't know. I don't think so." The voice trailed away. "If you don't really

....

mentioned it told me

Fourteen She will be fourteen years old

down the wash across the marsh; across the wet land

think George would freeze, then you want to find him because you think he killed Ernesto? Is that it? Or somebody thinks he killed Ernesto?"

"I guess somebody thinks he might have. Or that he was close enough to where it happened to have got a look at who did it. Me, I think he can tell me enough so we'll know what happened, and why it happened."

"I can't remember anything else," Susanne said. She glanced at him and then at her hands. She tugged the cuff down to her knuckles, looked at her fingernails, then hid them in fists, then put the fists in her pockets. Leaphorn let the silence last, looking at her. She was much too thin, he thought, the skin stretched too tight over fragile bones.

"There's a problem, though, if I don't find him. Or *maybe* there is. The way Shorty Bowlegs died was somebody hit him over the head in his hogan last night. Whoever it was was looking for something. Searched through everything in the hogan. O.K. Think about it a little bit. Somebody kills the Cata boy. Two days later somebody kills George's dad and searches George's hogan." He looked at her. "What do you think? I'm nervous about George. Two killings, very much alike, and George is the only thing that connects the two of them."

"You mean George's father was killed. And you think somebody might be . . ."

Leaphorn shrugged. "*Quién sabe?* His friend gets killed, George disappears, his daddy gets killed, what's next? It makes me nervous."

....

absently automatically; without thinking

Quién sabe? Who knows? (in Spanish)

"I didn't know his dad had been killed. I thought he just died."

"After George talked to you Monday, he went to their hogan. When Cecil got home Monday night, he found their horse was gone and their 30-30, and some of George's clothes. And George had left a note. He told Cecil he had some business with a kachina, or kachinas, and he was going to take care of it, and he'd be gone several days. Now, does that suggest anything to you? Did he say anything here about that?"

Susanne was frowning. "He was in a hurry. I remember that. Sweating like he'd been running." She squeezed her eyes shut, concentrating. "He said he wanted to get some **venison**. And when Halsey said no, George and I went out of the hogan. Then he started asking me about the Zuñi religion. I remember what he said, and what I said."

She opened her eyes and looked at Leaphorn. "I already told you that, about telling him I only knew what little Ted told me. And then he asked me if the Council of the Gods forgave people for breaking taboos. I said I didn't know anything about it. And then he said something about going to a dance hall, or to a dance, or something like that." She frowned again. "I think I must have misunderstood him. It sounded something like that, but that doesn't make much sense."

"Dance hall? I don't seem to . . ."

"It was something about a dance hall. I remember because I thought it sounded crazy at the time."

"I'll do some asking around," Leaphorn said. "Another

....

venison deer meat

thing. I don't think you should stay here anymore. I don't think it's safe."

"Why not?"

"It's not much more than just a feeling," Leaphorn said. "But George didn't have very many people close to him. And now two of them are dead. So that leaves you, and maybe Ted Isaacs, and as far as anybody knows, that's about all."

There was more to the feeling than that. There was the **hostility** of Halsey and Hair in Bun, and there was Mr. Baker grinning in the background, **smelling heroin in the wind**. And O'Malley's uncasual remark about low-flying planes. Whether or not Halsey's commune was **a cover for** delivery of Mexican narcotics flown up across the Sonoran desert, there were narcotics around. The condition of the man called Otis testified to that. It would be only a matter of time before Baker moved in.

"By the way," Leaphorn said. "How's Otis?"

"He's gone. Halsey took him into the bus station at Gallup yesterday."

"Was he better?"

"Maybe a little," Susanne said. "I don't think so." She paused. "Look," she said, "do you think Ted might be in any danger?"

"I don't know," Leaphorn said. "I wouldn't have figured Shorty Bowlegs was in any danger. Either somebody had a reason for killing him that we don't know about, or somebody was looking for George and he got in the way. To tell the truth,

....

hostility meanness, anger

smelling heroin in the wind believing that there was heroin involved in these murders

a cover for hiding

after that I'm nervous about *anybody* connected with George. That includes you."

"Have you warned Ted? You ought to warn him. Tell him to go back to Albuquerque. Tell him to get away from here." She looked **distraught**.

"I will," Leaphorn said. "I'm telling you, too. Get away from here."

"I can't," Susanne said. "But he could. There's no reason he can't."

"You can, too," Leaphorn said. "Go. What keeps you here?"

She moved her shoulders, opened her hands, a gesture of helplessness. "I don't have anyplace to go."

"Go back to your family."

"No. There isn't any family."

"Everybody's got a family. You said you had a parent. There must be grandparents, uncles." Leaphorn's Navajo mind struggled with the concept of a child with no family, found it incredible, and rejected it.

"No family," Susanne said. "My dad doesn't want me back." She said it without emotion, **a comment on the weather of the human heart**. "And the only grandmother I know about lives somewhere back east and doesn't speak to my dad and I've never seen her. And if I've got uncles I don't know about them."

Leaphorn **digested this in silence**.

"I guess *here's* my family," she said with a shaky laugh. "Halsey, and Grace and Bad Dude Arnett, and Lord Ben, and Pots, and Oats, until Oats left. That and the rest of them, that's

....

distraught nervous and upset

a comment on the weather of the human heart a casual remark

digested this in silence quietly listened

my family."

"You sleep with Halsey?"

"Sure," she said, **defiant**. "You **earn your keep**. Do some of the washing, and some of the cooking, and sleep with Halsey."

"He has the money, I guess. Made the deal with Frank Bob Madman for the allotment, and started this place, and buys the groceries."

"I think so. I don't know for sure. Anyway, I don't have any. I have these clothes I've got on, and a dress with a stain on the skirt, and another pair of jeans, and some underwear and a ballpoint pen. But I don't have any money."

"No money at all? Not enough for a bus ticket someplace?"

"I don't have a penny."

Leaphorn pushed himself away from the arroyo wall and looked downstream. No one **was in sight**.

"How about Ted Isaacs?" he said. "You like him. He likes you. You could sort of look after one another until I can find George."

"No."

"Why not?'

"I don't know why I talk to you like this," Susanne said. "I never talk to anyone like this. No, because Ted is going to marry me. Someday."

"Why not now?"

"He can't marry me now," Susanne said. "He's got to finish that project and when he does he'll be just about famous, and he'll get a good **faculty appointment**, and he'll have

....

defiant boldly

earn your keep work to stay here

was in sight could be seen

faculty appointment teaching job

everything he's never had before. No more being dirt poor and no more being nobody anybody ever heard of."

"O.K. Then why can't you just go over there and stay at his camper? I bet you don't eat much and you could help him dig."

"Dr. Reynolds wouldn't let him." She paused. "I used to work over there a lot, but Dr. Reynolds talked to Ted about it." Her expression said she hoped Leaphorn would understand this. "I'm not a professional, and I don't know anything about **excavation** really. It looks simple, but it's actually extremely complicated. And this is going to be a really important dig. It's going to make them rewrite all their books about Stone Age man, and I might mess something up. My just being there, **an amateur** who doesn't know anything, might make people wonder about how well it was done. And anyway, **the establishment** will be looking for things to criticize. So really, it's better if I stay away until it's finished." It came out with the sound of something memorized.

"Isaacs told you all that before we had two killings," Leaphorn said. "That sort of changes things. We'll go get your stuff and we don't need to tell Halsey anything except that I'm taking you with me."

"Halsey won't like it," Susanne said. But she followed him down the path.

....

excavation digging for artifacts

an amateur someone who is not an expert

the establishment those who believe in the old theory

BEFORE YOU MOVE ON...

1. **Inference** Why do you think Leaphorn asks Susanne what George knows about deer hunting?

2. **Summarize** Reread pages 118–119. Why won't Reynolds allow Susanne to live with Ted Isaacs?

LOOK AHEAD Read pages 120–130 to find out why Ted Isaacs is so determined to prove Reynolds's theory.

› **12** ‹

Wednesday, December 3, 3:48 P.M.

In another two or three minutes the lower edge of the red sun would sink behind the strata of clouds hanging over western Arizona. Now the oblique angle of its late afternoon rays were almost parallel to the slope of the hillside toward Zuñi Wash. They **projected** the moving shadow of Ted Isaacs almost a thousand feet down the hillside, and beside it stretched the motionless shadow of Lieutenant Joseph Leaphorn. Every juniper, every bushy yellow chamiso, every outcrop of stone streaked the yellow-gray of the autumn grass with a stripe of dark blue shadow. And beyond the hillside, beyond the gridwork of twine that marked the Isaacs dig, two miles across the valley, the great bulk of Corn Mountain loomed, its broken cliffs sharply outlined in the reds and pinks of reflected sunlight and the blacks of shadows. It was one of those moments of startling beauty **which as a matter of habit Joe Leaphorn took time to examine and savor.** But he was **preoccupied**.

"Oh, God damn it," Isaacs said. "God damn it to hell." He threw another shovelful of earth onto the sifter frame, slammed the shovel against the wheelbarrow, and wiped his forehead

....

projected showed
which as a matter of habit Joe Leaphorn took time to
examine and savor that Joe Leaphorn would stop to admire
preoccupied too busy with other things

against the back of his hairy forearm. He began working the dirt furiously through the wire, then threw down the trowel; sat on the edge of the sifter and looked at Leaphorn, his expression **belligerent**.

"I don't see how she could really be in any danger," he said. **"That's just sheer damned guesswork."** Isaacs' voice was angry. "Not even hardly guesswork. Just a sort of crazy **intuition**."

"I guess that's about right. Just a guess," Leaphorn said. He squatted now, sinking to his heels. A pair of golden eagles coasted down the air currents over the Zuñi River, hunting any rodent that moved. Leaphorn noted this without enjoying it. He found Isaacs' reaction interesting. Not what he expected.

Isaacs pinched the skin over the bridge of his nose between a grimy thumb and finger, shook his head. "George's dad got killed the same way Ernesto did, you say? Hit over the head." He shook his head again and then looked up at Leaphorn. "It does sound like somebody's crazy unless you can figure some reason for it." Across the slope toward Zuñi, smoke of supper cooking was beginning to make its evening haze over the hill that was Halona, the Middle Place of the World. "Maybe it's those goddamned Indians," Isaacs said. "Some kind of feud between the Zuñis and the Navajos, maybe. Could it be something like that?" His tone said he knew too much anthropology to believe it.

"No. Not likely," Leaphorn said. But he thought about it, as he had before. Would Ernesto's family strike out in revenge,

....

belligerent aggressive, argumentative
"That's just sheer damned guesswork." "You are only guessing she is in danger."
intuition feeling

presuming young Bowlegs had killed their son and nephew? From what Leaphorn knew of the Zuñi Way, such an act would be utterly unlikely. There hadn't been a homicide at Zuñi in modern times and damned few, Leaphorn suspected, in the history of these people. As far as he could remember, everything in their religion and philosophy **militated against** violence. Even **internal, unexpressed anger** was a taboo during their ceremonial periods, for it would destroy the effectiveness of rituals and weaken the tribal link with the supernatural. And when there had been some sort of killing, **way back somewhere in the dimness of time**, the Zuñis had settled the affair by arranging for gifts to be given the family that lost a member and having the guilty party initiated into the proper medicine society to cure him.

"I don't think there's any chance at all there's any revenge mixed up in this," he said. Still, if he didn't find George, if nothing cleared up this affair, then someday in the future he would try to learn if there had been a new initiation into whatever Zuñi cult would be responsible for curing the sickness of homicide. He probably wouldn't learn anything, but he would try.

"You really think maybe there's some danger for Susie?" Isaacs asked. "Look," he said. "I can't keep her here. Can't you put a guard out there, or something? Or put her someplace where she's safe? You're the law. You're supposed to keep people from getting hurt."

"I'm Navajo law and that gal's white, and I don't even know

....

militated against opposed

internal, unexpressed anger feeling angry

way back somewhere in the dimness of time a long time ago

for sure whether those hogans are on Navajo land. And even if I did know for sure, all I've got is an uneasy feeling. The way it works out, Susanne's just **not my baby**."

Isaacs stared at Leaphorn. "I think she'll be all right," he said. His face said he was trying hard to believe it.

"There's another thing, too. Just between us, it wouldn't surprise me any if there were some arrests out there one of these days soon. If she's out there, she's going to get herself **locked up**."

"Narcotics?"

"Probably."

"Those damned crazy bastards!"

"I thought maybe you wouldn't want her pulled in on that," Leaphorn said.

"I don't want her out there at all," Isaacs said. "But right now I can't do a goddamn thing. . . ." He stopped.

"Well," Leaphorn said. "I didn't mean to take up so much of your time. I just had the wrong impression." He got up, started to walk away. Isaacs' hand caught his elbow.

"Aren't you going to do anything about her? Look . . ."

"Yeah," Leaphorn said. "I'm going to go try to find George Bowlegs and try to get these killings cleared up. When that gets done you won't have to worry about her getting hit on the head. There's nothing I can do about getting her clear of **a narcotics raid**. In fact, I can think of a couple of people who'd be **pissed off** if they knew I was talking to anybody about it."

"I *wish* I could do something . . ." Isaacs' voice trailed off.

....

not my baby not my responsibility

locked up put in jail

a narcotics raid being arrested for drugs

pissed off angry

His expression was tortured.

"I sort of got the impression that she'd be willing to marry you," Leaphorn said. "That part of it's no business of mine, but then you could—"

The expression on Isaacs' face stopped him. Leaphorn shrugged. "O.K., forget it. I forget sometimes that white men got a different way of thinking about things than us Induns. One more thing: you're another one who might be in line for a hit on the head. You should—"

"Damn you," Isaacs said. His voice was barely under control. "What do you think? You think I don't care? You think I don't love her?" His voice was rising to a yell. "Let me tell you something, you **self-righteous** son of a bitch. I never had anything until Susie came by here last summer. I never had a girl, clothes, no money, no car, nor no time for women, and none of them would look at me twice anyway. And then here was Susie, ragged and all, and living at the commune, but you can tell what she is underneath all that. She's **quality**, that's what she is . . . quality. And you know what? Right from the first, we liked one another. She was fascinated by what we're doing here, and by God, she was fascinated by me." His tone suggested he couldn't believe this himself. "She couldn't stay away and I **couldn't stand it** if she did."

"But she did quit coming by here," Leaphorn said. "She hasn't been here in more than a week. You told me that, didn't you?"

Isaacs sat down again on the wheelbarrow, slumped, looking

....

self-righteous arrogant, proud
quality a good person
couldn't stand it would be unhappy

utterly tired and utterly defeated.

"That's something else you don't understand." He **indicated** the string-gridded dig site with a half-hearted wave. "About what this dig here is. We're proving the Reynolds theory here. I already told you that. But yesterday and today, I've been getting everything we dreamed we'd ever get. Not just the Folsom workshop chips mixed in with the parallel-flaked stuff. That was about as much as we'd ever dared hope for and I've been getting that all day. But we got **the hard evidence**, too." He pulled a handful of envelopes from his bulging shirt pocket. "I'm finding Folsom artifacts and parallel-flaked stuff coming out of the same blanks. It's more of that petrified marsh bamboo. Miocene stuff. Out of those formations south of Santa Fe." He spilled the contents of one of the envelopes onto his palm and extended it.

Three large pieces of flint and a score of chips and flakes, all pink or salmon-colored. Leaphorn leaned forward to examine it, noticing between the heavily callused ridges on Isaacs' palm an angry red blister, and noticing that the hand was shaking.

"Pick it up and take a close look," Isaacs said. "See that grain? Now look at this piece here. He was making something like what we've been calling a Yuma point out of this one." Isaacs' cracked, dirty fingernail indicated the series of ridges where the flint had been flaked away. "But he pressed too hard, or something, and his blank broke. So . . ." Isaacs fished another pinkish stone from his palm. "He started making this one. Notice the leaf shape? He had a rough-out Folsom point, but when he punched out the **fluting**, this one snapped, too."

....

utterly completely

indicated pointed to

the hard evidence solid proof

fluting groove, ridge

"Having a bad day," Leaphorn said.

"But look," Isaacs said. "Damn it. Use your eyes. Look at the grain in this petrified wood. It's the same. Notice the discoloration in this piece." He indicated with his fingernail a streak of dark red. "Notice how that same streak picks up in this one where he was trying to make the Folsom point. It's the very same damned piece of flint."

"It sure as hell looks like it. Can you prove it?"

"I'm sure a **mineralogist** with a microscope can prove it."

"You found them right together?"

"Right in the same grid," Isaacs said. He pointed to it. "Seventeen W, right there on the top of the ridge, right where a guy might be sitting watching for game down at the river while he chipped himself out some tools. And there was more of the same stuff in two of the adjoining grids. The guy must have broken one, dropped it right where he was sittin' there, and went to work on the other one."

"And broke it, and dropped it, too," Leaphorn said.

"And because he did, we blow the hell out of a tired old theory of Early Man and make anthropology admit the traditional disappearing man story **won't hold water** anymore."

"Has Reynolds got the good news yet?"

"Not until he comes back from Tucson this weekend," Isaacs said. "And that's what I was starting to explain to you. Reynolds is probably the one guy in the world who would give a graduate student **a break** like this. You probably know how it works. The professor who finds the site, and **scares up** the digging money,

....

mineralogist rock expert
won't hold water will not be believed
a break an opportunity
scares up gets

and plans the strategy—it's his dig. The graduate students do the shovel work and the sorting, but the professor makes all the decisions and he publishes the report under his name, and if his students are lucky, maybe he puts their names in a **footnote**, or maybe he doesn't. But with Reynolds, it's the other way around. He tells you how to do it and what to look for and he **turns you loose**. And then whatever you find you publish yourself. There's a dozen people around the country who have made their reputations that way because of him. He gives away the glory and all he expects in return is that you do him a scientific job." He looked at Leaphorn, his face bleak. "By that I mean a perfect job. Perfect."

"What do you mean?"

"I mean you don't make a single mistake. You don't **screw up anything**. Your records are exactly right. Nothing happens that would let any other scientist in any way cast any doubt on what you've found." Isaacs laughed, a grim, manufactured sound. "Like you don't let a couple of kids hang around your dig site. Like you don't let a girl hang around. You work from daylight until dark seven days a week and you don't let a damn thing distract you."

"I see," Leaphorn said.

"Reynolds let me know he was disappointed when he saw Susie here," Isaacs said. "And he **raised bloody hell** over the boys."

"So that sort of gives you a choice between Reynolds, who's done you a bunch of favors, and that girl, who needs some help."

....

footnote note at the bottom of the page
turns you loose lets you do it yourself
screw up anything make a mistake
raised bloody hell was extremely angry

"No. That's not it." Isaacs sat on the wheelbarrow rim. He looked away from Leaphorn, out across the valley. The sun had dipped behind the cloudbank now and the breeze was suddenly picking up. It riffled through his hair.

"These rocks I got here mean the rest of my life," he said slowly. "It means I get past the Ph.D. committee with no sweat, and I get the degree. And instead of being one of a hundred new Ph.D.s fighting it out for maybe three or four decent faculty places around the country, I have my pick. I have the reputation, and a book to write, and the status. And when I walk into the American Anthropological Association meetings, instead of being some **grubby little pissant of a** graduate assistant at some little junior college, why, I'm the man who helped **fill in the missing link**. It's the kind of thing that lasts you all of your life."

"All I was suggesting that you do," Leaphorn said, "was bring Susanne here and keep an eye on her until this business settles down."

Isaacs still stared out toward the Zuñi Buttes. "I thought about it before. Just to get her away from that place. But here's the way it would work. Reynolds would figure it was the last proof he needed that I wasn't the man for this dig. He'd pull me off and put somebody else on it. He may do it anyway because of those boys being here. And that would **blow** my dissertation research, and the degree, and **the whole ball game**."

He swung toward Leaphorn, his anger blazing again. "Look," he said. "I don't know how it was with you. Maybe

---

grubby litte pissant of a unimportant, insignificant

fill in the missing link find the important artifact

blow ruin

the whole ball game my career; everything

pretty thin. Well, my folks, such as I had, were all east Tennessee **white trash**. Never been a one of them went to college. Never a one had **a pot to piss in**. Just poor trash. My dad had run off somewhere, according to my mother, and I wouldn't even swear she knew who he was. With me it was living with a drunken uncle in a sharecropper shack, and chopping cotton, and every year pleading for him to let me go back to school when fall got there so I could finish high school. And after that being janitor and dishwasher in a frat house at Memphis State, and even trying to get into the army just to get onto the GI Bill and find out what it was like to eat regular." Isaacs fell suddenly silent, thinking about it.

"You know how long I been shoveling out here? Damn near six months. I get out here by the time the light gets good enough. And I'm digging until dark. Reynolds got a three-thousand-dollar grant and he split it among eight sites. This one's sprawled out all up and down this hill so he gave me a little more. He gave me four hundred dollars. And I borrow money here and there and buy that old truck and build the cabin on it and try to keep eating on about fifty dollars a month and hope to God the **loan sharks** won't figure out where I am and take the truck back. And I don't **begrudge** a minute of it because this is the first chance an Isaacs had to be anything but dirt." Isaacs stopped. He was still staring at Leaphorn, his jaw muscles working. "And when I get it made, I'm going to take about two thousand dollars or whatever it costs and I'm going to get these beaver teeth pushed back into my face. It's the sort

----

white trash poor, white people
a pot to piss in any money
loan sharks people who loaned me money
begrudge regret; feel bad about

of thing that you get done when you're about twelve years old, if anybody gives a damn, and it's probably too late now to fix 'em, but by God, by God, I'm going to try."

On his way back down the slope Leaphorn noticed that Susanne was no longer waiting in the carryall. It didn't surprise him. Even watching his conversation with Isaacs from a distance, it would have been easy enough for the girl to see that she'd guessed right—that Ted Isaacs wasn't eager to have her move in. So she hadn't waited for the embarrassment of hearing about it. Leaphorn thought about where the girl might have gone and about all the things that go into choices. He thought about how the whiteman mind of Ted Isaacs **sorted things out** so that Susanne was on one side of the scale and everything else he wanted on the other, and about **the weighting of values** that would cause Susanne to be rejected. Then he shook his head and changed the theme. He **skipped back** nine thousand years to a naked hunter squatting on Isaacs' ridge, laboriously chipping out a lance point, breaking it, calmly dropping it, working on another one, breaking it, calmly dropping it. Leaphorn had trouble with the second part of this scene. His imagination insisted on having his Folsom Man shout an angry Stone Age curse and throw the offending flint down the slope. Way down the slope where no anthropologist would find it ninety centuries later.

....

sorted things out thought about things

the weighting of values the way he judged what was important

skipped back let his thoughts go back

BEFORE YOU MOVE ON...

1. **Cause and Effect** What will happen to Isaacs if he proves Reynolds's theory?

2. **Summarize** Isaacs describes his archeological find to Leaphorn. Why does his explanation bother Leaphorn?

LOOK AHEAD Read pages 131–145 to find out why the Zuñis are so secretive.

≫ **13** ≪

Wednesday, December 3, 5 P.M.

Father Ingles of the Order of Saint Francis was a **wiry**, tidy, tough-looking little man, his face a background of old **pockmarks** overlaid with two generations of damage by sun and wind. Leaphorn found him sitting on the low wall surrounding the cemetery behind the Saint Anthony's Mission church. He was talking to a youngish Zuñi. "Be with you in a minute," Father Ingles said. He and the Zuñi finished working down a list of names—members of the Catholic Youth Organization girls' basketball team who would be making the bus trip to Gallup to meet the Navajo Sawmill Jills and the Acoma Bravettes in a holiday tournament. Now, with that job finished and the Zuñi gone, he still sat on the wall, huddled in a **castoff navy windbreaker**, looking across the graves at nothing in particular and telling Leaphorn in a slow, soft voice what he knew of the Shorty Bowlegs family.

Leaphorn knew Ingles by reputation. He had worked for years out of Saint Michael's Mission near Window Rock and was known among the Window Rock Navajos as Narrowbutt **in deference to** his bony hindquarters. He spoke Navajo,

....

wiry lean and muscular
pockmarks scars left by pimples
castoff navy windbreaker old, blue jacket
in deference to because of

which was rare among white men, and had mastered its complex **tonalities** so thoroughly that he could practice the Navajo pastime of **spinning off puns** and absurdities by pretending to slightly mispronounce his verbs. Now he talked somberly. He had told Leaphorn about the family of Ernesto Cata, and now he told him about Shorty Bowlegs. Much of this Leaphorn already knew. After a while, when enough time had passed to make this conversation absolutely comfortable, Leaphorn would ask the questions he had come to ask. Now he was content to listen. It was something Joe Leaphorn did very well.

"This George, now. He's an aggravating little devil," Ingles was saying. "I don't think I ever saw a kid with a **funnier turn of mind**. Quick. Quick. Quick. About half genius and half crazy. The kind of a boy that if you can make a Christian out of him will make you a saint. Full of mysticism—most of it nonsense and all muddled up—but something in him driving him to know more than a natural man is supposed to know. He'll probably end up writing poetry, or shooting himself, or being a drunk like his father. Or maybe we'll still bag him and we'll have a Saint Bowlegs of Zuñi."

"Had he been coming to church here?"

"For a while," Ingles said. He laughed. "I guess you'd say he studied us, **in competition** with witchcraft and sorcery and the Zuñi religion and plain old starve-a-vision mysticism." The priest frowned. "You know, I'm not being fair to the boy, talking about him like this. George was looking for something because he was smart enough to see he didn't have anything.

....

tonalities sounds
spinning off puns telling jokes
funnier turn of mind more unusual way of thinking
in competition along

132

He knew all about what his mother had done and that's a cruel thing for a child. And of course he could see his dad was a drunk, and maybe that's even worse. He was away from his family, so he was denied the Navajo Way, and he didn't have anything to replace it."

"What did he know about his mother?"

"I've heard two **variations**. They lived over around Coyote Canyon someplace with her **outfit**. One way, she took to hitching rides into Gallup for drinking bouts with men. Or she moved out on Bowlegs and in with two brothers—and they were supposed to be witches. Take your pick. Or mix 'em up and take what you like of both. Anyway, Bowlegs didn't get along with his wife's people so he came back to his own folks at Ramah and then he got a job over here herding Zuñi sheep."

"Let's skip back just a little. You said the gossip was she moved in with two brothers who were witches. You remember any more about that? Who said it? Anything at all specific?"

"Guess I heard it two or three places. You know how gossip is. All **fifth or sixth hand**, and who knows where it started?" Ingles peered out across the cemetery, thinking. Moments passed. Ingles had lived among Navajos long enough to let time pass without **strain**. He fished a cigar out of his inside shirt pocket, offered it wordlessly to Leaphorn, who shook his head, bit off the tip, lit it, and exhaled a thin blue plume of smoke into the evening air. "Can't remember anything specific," he said. "Just that somebody told me the boy's mother was living with a couple of witches. You think it might be important?"

....

variations different stories
outfit gang; group of people
fifth or sixth hand told by someone else
strain discomfort

"No," Leaphorn said. "I just make a point not to **overlook witch talk** like that. We don't have much trouble on the reservation, but that's where a lot of it starts."

"You believe in witches?"

"That's like me asking you if you believe in sin, Father," Leaphorn said. "The point is you gradually learn that witch talk and trouble sort of go together."

"I've noticed that myself," Ingles said. "You think there's a connection here?"

"I don't see how."

Ingles ejected another blue plume into the air. They watched it drift down the wall. "Anyway, by then George's dad was going after the bottle pretty hard and so maybe George's interest in coming around the church was just running away from drinking. Anyway, he didn't stay interested long."

"You didn't get him baptized?"

"No. From what Ernesto told me, George started getting interested in the Zuñi Way instead. Comparing their **origin myth** with the Navajo and with our Genesis, that sort of thing. Ernesto used to bring him in to talk to me. He'd ask me about the difference between the Zuñi kachina and our saints. Things like that."

Father Ingles **punctuated** another silence with more smoke.

"Very similar in a way. As we see it, when a Christian completes the good life his soul joins the community of saints. When the Zuñi completes his path, his spirit joins the village of the kachinas and he becomes one of them."

....

overlook witch talk ignore conversations about witches

origin myth story about how the world was created

punctuated interrupted

"What I know of the Zuñi religion is a little bit out of the anthropology books, a little **hearsay**, and a little from a roommate I used to have. It's not much, and part of it's probably wrong."

"Probably," Ingles said. "The Zuñis found out a long time ago that some outsiders looked on their religion as **a sort of side show**. And after that, most of them wouldn't talk about it to the anthropologists, and some of those who did **were deliberately misleading**."

"Right now I wish *I* knew a little more about it," Leaphorn said. "George told his little brother that he was going to find a kachina, or maybe it was *some kachinas*. He didn't seem to know exactly where to find them, but he must have had some idea because he said he'd be gone several days."

Ingles frowned. "Find some kachinas? He couldn't have meant the kachina dolls, I guess?"

"I don't think so. I think he, or he and Ernesto together, had done something to offend the kachinas—or thought they had, or some crazy damn thing like that—and George wanted to do something about it."

Ingles laughed. "That sounds about like George," he said. "That sounds exactly like him." He shook his head. "But where would he go? Did he say anything else?"

"He said if he didn't get his business done, he'd have to come back to Zuñi for Shalako. And he took one of the Bowlegs horses, if that helps any, and their rifle. To kill a deer for eating, I'd guess. And a girl he knew told me he said something about

....

hearsay rumor
a sort of side show entertainment
were deliberately misleading lied about it

going to a dance hall. Can you make any connection out of all that?"

Ingles made a clucking sound with his tongue against his teeth. "You know what it might be?" he said. "It might be he's trying to find Kothluwalawa." The priest laughed and shook his head. "I don't know whether that makes any sense, but with George sense isn't all that important."

"Kothluwalawa?" Leaphorn asked. "Where's that?" The priest's amusement irritated him. "He was going somewhere you can go on a horse."

Ingles sensed the anger. "It's really not as impossible as it sounds. We tend to think of heaven as being up in the sky. The Zuñis also have **a geographical concept for it**, because of the nature of their mythology. Do you know that myth?"

"If I did, I don't remember much of it now."

"It's part of the **migration mythology**. The Zuñis had completed their emergence up through the four underworlds and had started their great journey hunting for the Middle Place of the Universe. Some children of the Wood Fraternity were carried across the Zuñi River by the older people. There was sort of a panic and the children were dropped. As they were washed downstream, instead of drowning they turned into water animals—frogs, snakes, tadpoles, so forth—and they swam downstream to this place we're talking about. According to the mythology, it's a lake. Once they got there, the children changed from water animals and became kachinas, and they formed the Council of the Gods—the Rain God of the North,

....

a geographical concept for it a location on Earth

migration mythology ancient story of the wanderings of the
Zuñi people

136

the Rain God of the South, the Little Fire God, and the rest of them. Originally a hundred or so, I think."

"Sort of like the Holy People of the Navajo," Leaphorn said.

"Not really. Your Holy People—Monster Slayer, Changing Woman, Born of Water, and all that—they're more like a cross between the Greek hero idea and the lesser Greek gods. More human than **divine**, you know. The kachinas aren't like anything in Navajo or white culture. We don't have a word for this concept, and neither do you. They're not gods. The Zuñi have only one God, Awonawilona, who was the creator. And then they have Shiwanni and Shinwanokia—a man-and-woman team created by God to create the Sun, and Mother Earth, and all living things. But the kachinas are different. Maybe you could call them ancestor spirits. Their attitude toward humans is friendly, fatherly. They bring blessings. They appear as rain clouds."

"I'd heard some of that," Leaphorn said. "So this Kothluwalawa where Bowlegs said he was going is a lake somewhere down the Zuñi Wash?"

"It's not that simple," Ingles said. "I have four books about the Zuñis in my office—each one written by **an ethnologist** or anthropologist who was an **authority**. They have it located in four different places. One of them has it down near the **confluence** of Zuñi Wash and the Little Colorado, over in Arizona, not far from Saint Johns. And one of them says it's down south near the old Ojo Caliente village. And another of them puts it up in the Nutria Lake area northeast of here. And

----

divine gods
an ethnologist a scientist who studies races of people
authority expert
confluence joining place

I've heard a couple of other places, most often a little natural lake just across the Arizona border. And I know that *some* Zuñis think of it as being located only in **metaphysics**, beyond time and space."

Leaphorn said nothing.

"What made me think of Kothluwalawa was that business of the dance hall. If you translate that word to English it means something like 'Dance Hall of the Dead,' or maybe 'Dance Ground of the Spirits,' or something like that." Ingles smiled. "Rather a poetic concept. In life, ritual dancing for the Zuñi is sort of a perfect expression of . . ." He paused, searching for the word. "Call it ecstasy, or joy, or life, or community unity. So what do you do when you're beyond life, with no labors to perform? You spend your time dancing."

The priest blew another blue cloud of cigar smoke over the cemetery, and they sat there, Navajo policeman and Franciscan missionary, watching the cloud **dissipate** over the Zuñi graves. In the west the sky had turned garish with sunset. What George Bowlegs was hunting, Leaphorn thought, was a concept so foreign to The People that their language lacked a word for it. There was no heaven in the Navajo cosmos, and no friendly kachina spirit, and no pleasant life after death. If one was lucky, there was **oblivion**. But for most, there was the unhappy malevolent ghost, the chindi, wailing away **the eons** in the darkness, spreading sickness and evil. He thought about what Ingles had said. This Kothluwalawa might be the word Cecil remembered that started with a *K*.

....

metaphysics theory
dissipate break apart and disappear
oblivion nothingness
the eons forever, eternity

"I think what's important is not where this Zuñi heaven is located," Leaphorn said. "What's important is where George thinks it's located."

"Yes," Ingles said. "The same thought occurred to me."

"Where would he think it is?"

Ingles thought about it. "I bet I know. I bet it would be that little lake just across the border. It's used a lot for religious purposes. The religious people make **prayer retreats** to shrines over there, and they go several times a year to catch frogs and so forth. I think it would be my first guess. If George was asking around about it, that's where he'd most likely be told it was located. And now I have a question for you. Why are you hunting the boy? Do you think he killed Ernesto and his own father, too? If you think that, then I think you're wrong."

Leaphorn thought about the answer. "He could have killed Cata. He must have been somewhere near when it happened. And then he ran. And he *could* have killed Shorty. But there doesn't seem to be any reason. I guess that's the trouble. Nobody seems to have a reason." Leaphorn's tone made a question. He looked at the priest.

"To kill Ernesto? Not that I know anything about," Ingles said. "He was a good kid. **Served Mass** for me. Had a lot of friends. No enemies that I know of. What kid that age has enemies? They're too young for that."

"Cecil Bowlegs told me that Ernesto and George had stolen something." Leaphorn spoke slowly. This was the sensitive point. It had to be said very carefully. "It was supposed to have

....

prayer retreats trips to pray

Served Mass Was part of the Catholic ceremonies

been something from that anthropological dig north of Corn Mountain. Ernesto was a Catholic. He was an altar boy. If he stole something he knew he had to give it back before he could make a good confession. Is that right?"

Ingles was grinning at him. "What you are saying is, 'You're **his confessor**. Did he confess anything to you that would explain why somebody killed him?' That's what you are asking me, but you know I can't reveal what I'm told in the confessional."

"But Cata's dead now. Nothing you tell me now is going to hurt that boy. Maybe it would help George Bowlegs."

"I'm thinking about it," Ingles said. "You know, I've been a priest almost forty years and it never came up before. Probably I won't tell you anything, but let's think a minute about **the theology we've got ourselves involved in here**."

"Just **negative information might help**. Just knowing that he didn't steal anything important. Cecil Bowlegs told me it was some arrowheads from the dig site, but it wasn't that. They checked and told me they weren't missing any artifacts. In fact, they weren't missing anything."

Ingles sat silently, his teeth worrying his lower lip, his mind worrying the problem. "To be a mortal sin, the offense has to be serious," he said. "What you're describing wouldn't have been more than a very minor imperfection. Something a boy would do. Something a boy with a less scrupulous conscience than Ernesto wouldn't even think of confessing."

"Now he's dead can't you tell me?" Leaphorn said. "A tool?

....

his confessor the person he tells his sins to

the theology we've got ourselves involved in here this interesting religious question

negative information might help tell me what he didn't do

140

A piece of paper? Can you tell me what?"

"I think I can't," Ingles said. "Probably I shouldn't even tell you that it was **inconsequential**. Nothing of value. Nothing that would tell you anything at all."

"I wonder why, then, he wanted to confess it. Did *he* think it was important?"

"No. Not really. It was Saturday afternoon. I was hearing confessions. Ernesto wanted to talk to me, very privately, about something else. So he got in line. And then, since he was in the confessional anyway, I heard his confession and gave him absolution. Confession is a **sacrament**," Ingles explained. "God gives you grace for it, even if there's no sin to be **absolved**."

"Saturday. Last Saturday? The day before he was killed?"

"Yes," Father Ingles said. "Last Saturday. He was my **server** Sunday at Mass, but I didn't talk to him. That was the last time Ernesto and I had a talk."

Ingles slid suddenly from the wall. "I'm getting cold," he said. "Let's go in."

Through the heavy wooden door, Ingles bowed in the direction of the altar and pointed Leaphorn toward the back pew.

"I don't know what I've said that's helpful," he said. "That George Bowlegs' dad was a drunk which I guess you already knew. That Ernesto Cata hadn't done anything bad enough to cause anyone to kill him—or even scold him much, for that matter."

"Would it help any if you told me what Cata wanted to talk

---

inconsequential not important

sacrament Christian ceremonial practice

absolved forgiven

server altar boy

to you about? I mean before he confessed his sins?"

Ingles chuckled. "I doubt it," he said. "It was hardly the material for murder."

"But could you tell me what it was?"

"I don't think I'd tell a Zuñi," Ingles said. "But you're a Navajo." He smiled. "Ernesto thought maybe he had **violated** a Zuñi taboo. But he wasn't sure, and he was nervous about it, and he didn't want to admit anything to anyone in his kiva yet, and he just wanted to talk to a friend about it," Ingles said. "I was that friend."

"What taboo?"

"Children . . . anyone not yet old enough to be initiated into the Zuñi religion society aren't supposed to be told about the personifiers," Ingles said. "You know about that?"

"Something about it."

"Well, in Zuñi mythology, the Council of the Gods—or whatever you want to call the spirits of those drowned children—would come back to the village each year. They'd bring rain, crops, blessings of all sorts, dance with the people, and teach them the right way of doing things. But it always happened that some of the Zuñis would follow them when they left to return to the Dance Hall of the Dead. And when you followed, you died. This was too bad, and the kachinas didn't want it to keep happening, so they told the Zuñis that they would come no more. Instead the Zuñis should make sacred masks representing them, and valuable men of the kivas and the various fetish societies would be selected to **impersonate**

---

violated broken
impersonate pretend they were

142

various spirits. The kachinas would come only in spirit. They would be visible, I've been told, to certain sorcerers. But anyone else who saw them would die. Now, this arrangement between the kachinas and the Zuñis was a secret arrangement. Only those initiated into the religion were to know of it. The children were not to be told."

Leaphorn's attention had been split. He heard Ingles' slow, precise voice, but his eyes were studying the **murals** that spread down the walls of the mission. Against the blank white plaster were the Dancing Gods of the Zuñis, most of them man-sized and manlike, except for the **grotesque** masks, which gave them heads like monstrous birds. Only one was smaller, a figure of black spotted with red, and one was much larger—just over their heads by the railing of the choir loft was the giant figure of the Shalako, a nine-foot-high pyramid topped by a tiny head and supported by human legs. This was the "messenger bird" of the gods.

"That's what Ernesto was worried about," Ingles was saying. "He'd told George that he would be the personifier of Shulawitsi and he was worrying about whether that had broken the taboo. There." The priest pointed at the small black figure leading the **procession** of kachinas down the wall. "The little black one in the spotted mask is Shulawitsi, the Little Fire God. He's always impersonated by a boy. It's terribly hard work— exercises, running, physical conditioning, memorizing chants, memorizing dances. It's the highest possible honor a child can receive from his people, but it's **an ordeal**. They miss a

....

murals paintings
grotesque ugly
procession group
an ordeal a long, hard experience

lot of school."

"Telling George about it—*had* that violated the taboo?"

"I don't know, really," Father Ingles said. "George would have been initiated two or three years ago if he was a Zuñi—so he wasn't a child in the way the myth means and he certainly would have already known that kachinas in the Shalako ceremonials are being impersonated by the men who live here. But on the other hand, he hadn't been formally initiated into the cult secrets. The way it's explained in the myth, this Zuñi boy tells the little children deliberately, to **spoil** the ceremonial for them, because he's angry—and the anger is part of the taboo violation. It is forbidden to **harbor** any anger in any period of ceremonialism. Anyway, the Council of the Gods send the Salamobia to punish the boy." Ingles pointed to the fourth kachina in the mural—a muscular figure armed with a whip of yucca, its beaked head surmounted by a pointed plume of feathers, its eyes ferocious. Leaphorn's eyes had lingered on it earlier, caught by something familiar. Now he knew what it was. This was the same beaked mask he had seen two nights earlier, reflecting the moonlight behind the hogan at Jason's Fleece.

"What was the punishment?" Leaphorn asked.

"The Salamobia chopped off his head with a machete—right in the plaza out here—and played football with it." Ingles laughed. "Most of the Zuñi mythology is humane and gentle, but that one's as bad as one of the **Grimms' fairy tales**."

"Do you know how Ernesto was killed?"

....

spoil ruin

harbor feel

Grimms' fairy tales children's tales known for being dark and violent

Ingles looked surprised. "He bled to death, didn't he? I **presumed** he'd been knifed."

"Someone chopped him across the neck with a machete," Leaphorn said. "They almost cut his head off."

....

presumed thought

BEFORE YOU MOVE ON...

1. **Paraphrase** Reread page 135. Why do the Zuñis avoid sharing their religion with outsiders? How do they protect it?

2. **Plot** According to the myth, what does the Salamobia do to those who violate a taboo? Why could this fact be a clue?

LOOK AHEAD Read pages 146–161 to find out why Leaphorn returns to Shorty Bowleg's home.

» **14** «

Leaphorn had been up since dawn, making his third visit to
the Bowlegs hogan. Around the brush corral he had examined
the hoofprints of the horse George Bowlegs had taken,
memorizing the nature of the horseshoes and every split and
crack in the hooves. The body of Shorty Bowlegs was gone now.
Buried by one of the Zuñis for whom he had herded, Leaphorn
guessed, or taken by O'Malley for whatever **post-mortem
magic** the FBI laboratory technologists might wish to perform
in Albuquerque. The **livestock was** gone, too, but the **worldly
goods** of Shorty Bowlegs remained inside—made untouchable
to Navajos by ghost sickness. Their disarray had been increased
by a third search, this one by the federals.

Leaphorn stood at the doorway and thoughtfully inspected
the jumble. Something held him here—a feeling that he
was forgetting something, or overlooking something, leaving
something undone. But whatever it was, it eluded him now. He
wondered if O'Malley had found anything informative. If the
case broke and the Albuquerque FBI office issued a statement
explaining how the arrest had been made, Leaphorn wouldn't

----

post-mortem magic examination of the dead body

livestock was animals were

worldly goods possessions, things

the jumble Shorty's possessions

be told. He'd read about it in the Albuquerque *Journal* or the Gallup *Independent*. Leaphorn considered this fact without rancor as something natural as the turn of the seasons. At the moment six law-enforcement agencies were interested in the affair at Zuñi (if one counted the Bureau of Indian Affairs Law and Order Division, which was watching passively). **Each would function as its interests dictated that it must.** Leaphorn himself, without conscious thought, would influence his actions to the benefit of the Dinee if Navajo interests were at stake. Orange Naranjo, he knew, would do his work honestly and faithfully with full awareness that his good friend and employer, the sheriff of McKinley County, was seeking reelection. Pasquaanti was responsible first to laws centuries older than the whiteman's written codes. Highsmith, whose real job was traffic safety, would do as little as possible. And O'Malley would make his decisions with that ingrained FBI awareness that the rewards lay in good publicity, and the sensible attitude that other agencies were competitors for that publicity.

Leaphorn wasted a few moments considering why the FBI would accept jurisdiction in such a chancy affair. Usually the FBI would move into **marginal areas** only if someone somewhere was sure **his batting average could be helped by a successful prosecution.** Or if the case involved whatever held high agency priority of the season—and that these days would be either radical politics or narcotics. The presence of Baker said narcotics figured somewhere, and the attitude of

....

Each would function as its interests dictated that it must. Each agency had a different interest in the case.

marginal areas less important areas

his batting average could be helped by a successful prosecution it would help his career

O'Malley seemed to suggest that Baker had leads the federals weren't willing to share. Leaphorn **pondered** what these leads might be, **drew a total blank**, climbed back into his carryall, and started the motor. Behind him, in the rear-view mirror, he noticed the plank door of Shorty Bowlegs' hogan move. Shorty's malicious ghost, perhaps, or just the same gusty morning breeze that whipped an eddy of dust around the logs.

Following the directions Father Ingles had given him, Leaphorn picked up the gravel road that led to the Zuñi Tribal Sawmill back in the Cibola National Forest, continued on it to the Fence Lake road, turned northward past the prehistoric Yellow House Ruins to N.M. 53. The highway, as usual, was empty. As he approached the Black Rock airstrip a single-engine plane took off, banked above the highway in front of him, and climbed over Corn Mountain, heading eastward. Passing through the old village of Zuñi he slowed, thinking he might make the three-block detour to the Zuñi police station to learn if anything had developed overnight. **He suppressed the impulse.** If anything important had happened, it would have been known at the communications center at the Ramah chapter house, where he had spent the night. And he wasn't in the mood for talking to O'Malley or to Baker, or to Pasquaanti, or to anyone. O'Malley had told him to find Bowlegs. He would find Bowlegs if he could because **his curiosity demanded it**. And now for the first time since he'd been here there was something to work on. A direction. George had left his family hogan with the horse Monday night. The distance to

---

pondered thought about

drew a total blank could not figure it out

He suppressed the impulse. He decided not to go.

his curiosity demanded it he was curious

the lake would be maybe fifty miles. If George had taken the most direct route he would angle across the Zuñi reservation, probably pick up the Zuñi Wash about at the Arizona state line, and then follow this southwestward toward U.S. Highway 666. The country was rough, sloping irregularly away from the Continental Divide, which rose to almost eight thousand feet east of the reservation, toward that great inland depression which the maps called the Painted Desert. But the only barriers were natural ones. No more than two or three fences, Leaphorn guessed, in a day-and-a-half horseback ride.

Leaphorn's plan was simple. He would drive as close as he could get to the location of the lake and then begin looking for Bowlegs' tracks. He felt good about it, anticipating the pleasure of some solid accomplishment after three days of frustrations.

On the radio, a slightly nasal disk jockey was promoting a sky-diving exhibition at the Yah-Ta-Hey Trading Post and playing country-western records. Leaphorn flicked the tuning knob, got a **guttural** voice speaking alternately in English and Apache. He listened a moment, picking up an occasional word. It was a preacher from the San Carlos Apache reservation, one hundred miles to the south. "The good book says it to us," the man was saying. "**The inheritance of the sinner is as** the waterless desert." Leaphorn turned down the volume. A good line, he thought, for a year of drought.

The narrow **asphalt** narrowed even more, its gravel shoulders turning to weeds, and N.M. 53 abruptly became Arizona 61 at the border. Something was nagging at the corner

....

guttural deep

The inheritance of the sinner is as What bad people get when they die is like

asphalt road

of Leaphorn's consciousness, a vague thought which evaporated when he tried to capture it. It made him **uneasy**.

At the intersection with U.S. Highway 666, Leaphorn saw Susanne. She was standing north of the junction, a flour sack on the ground beside her, looking small and cold and frail, and pretending—after the first quick glance—not to notice the Navajo Police carryall. Leaphorn hesitated. He didn't want company today. He had looked forward to a day alone to restore the spirit. On the other hand, he was curious. And he **found himself remarkably fond of this girl**. He didn't want her to simply disappear. He pulled the carryall off the pavement and stopped beside her.

"Where you going?"

"I'm **hitchhiking**," she said.

"I see that. But where?"

"North. Up to Interstate Forty." She shook her head. "I guess I don't really know exactly. I'm going to decide whether to go east or west after I get to the Interstate."

"I think I know how to find George," Leaphorn said. "That's where I'm going now. To try. If you've got time you could help."

"I couldn't help."

"You're his friend," Leaphorn said. "He's almost certain to see me before I see him. He'll figure I'm after him so he'll hide. But if he sees you, he'll know it's all right."

"I wish I was sure it was all right myself," she said. But when he opened the door, she put the flour sack behind the seat and got into the cab beside him. He did a U-turn and started

....

uneasy feel uncomfortable

found himself remarkably fond of this girl really liked and cared about Susanne

hitchhiking trying to find someone to give me a ride

southward down 666. The sign at the intersection said ST. JOHNS 29 MILES.

"We're going south toward the place where Zuñi Wash goes under the highway," Leaphorn said. "About fifteen or sixteen miles. Before we get there, there's a ranch gate. We're going to pull in there and put this truck out of the way someplace **handy**, and then do some walking."

Susanne said nothing. The hilltop view stretched twenty miles. The country was mostly **undulating hills**, but far to the south the great tableland of the Zuñi reservation extended, broken low mesas with scrubby brush timber on top and barren erosion below.

As he had guessed, Susanne had had no breakfast. He pointed to the grocery sack he had picked up at the store in Ramah.

"What happened to you yesterday? When Isaacs came to talk to you, you were gone."

"I went back to the commune. It was just the way I told you, wasn't it? Ted couldn't do anything? And my being there just made it harder for him?"

Leaphorn decided not to comment on that.

"So why did you change your mind about staying at the commune?"

"Halsey changed it for me. He said I was attracting too much police."

He noticed she was eating hungrily. Not just no breakfast, he thought. Probably no supper, either. She had folded up the

....

handy convenient, nearby
undulating hills lots of hills

cuff of her denim shirt and from it the frayed gray sleeve of a wool undershirt extended, covering the back of her narrow, fragile hand. As she ate, rapidly and wordlessly, Leaphorn saw that the skin between the thumb and forefinger of her right hand bore the puckered white of old scar tissue. It was an ugly, disfiguring shape. Whatever had caused it had burned through the skin right into the muscle fiber.

"So Halsey **kicked you out**?"

"He said to get my stuff together and this morning he gave me a ride out to the highway." She looked out of the window, away from him. "I was right about Ted, wasn't I? There wasn't anything he could do."

"You were right about that situation," he said. "Isaacs explained it the same way you did. He said Reynolds would fire him if anybody stayed there with him."

"There's just no way he could possibly do it," she said. "This is Ted's really big hope. He's going to be famous after this. You know, he's never been nothing but poor. Him and his whole family. And this is Ted's chance. He's never had a thing."

It sounded, Leaphorn thought, as if Susanne was trying to **persuade** both of them.

"He just couldn't do it," she said. "No way he could do it."

Leaphorn found the ranch gate Father Ingles had described about a mile and a half up the slope from Zuñi Wash. A weather-bleached sign was nailed to the post. The message it had once proclaimed—"Posted, Keep Out" or "Shut the Gate"—had long since been erased by the sandblasting of

....

cuff sleeve
kicked you out made you leave
persuade convince

spring dust storms. Three coyote skins hung beside it, the gray dead hair riffling in the breeze.

"Why do they do that?" Susanne asked. "Stick 'em up on the fence?"

"The coyotes? I guess it's for the same reason white men put an animal's head on their wall. Shows everybody you got the **machismo** to kill him." The Navajo word for Hosteen Coyote was *ma ii*. He was the trickster, the joker, the subject of a thousand Navajo jokes, children's stories, and myths. He was often man's ally in the struggle to survive, and always the **bane** of a society which herded sheep. A Navajo would kill a lamb-killer if he could. It was a deed done with proper apology—not something to be **flaunted** on a roadside fence.

Leaphorn drove very slowly, keeping his wheels off the dirt track to cut the risk of raising dust. Each time the track branched toward another stock-watering windmill or a salt drop, Leaphorn chose the route that led toward the low escarpment of the Zuñi plateau. Father Ingles had said the lake was five or six miles in from the highway and below the mesa. It was a smallish natural playa that filled with draining runoff water in the rainy season and then dried slowly until the snow melt **recharged it** in the spring. Finding it would be relatively easy in a country where deer, antelope, and cattle trails would lead to any standing water.

The last dim trail dead-ended at a rusty windmill. Leaphorn pulled the carryall past it into a shallow arroyo and parked it amid a tangle of junipers.

....

machismo toughness, manliness
bane curse
flaunted shown in a bragging manner
recharged it filled it again

The lake proved to be less than a mile away. Leaphorn stood among the rocks on the ridge above it and examined it carefully through his binoculars. Except for a killdeer hopping on its stiltlike legs in the shallows, nothing moved anywhere around the cracked mud shore. Leaphorn studied the landscape **methodically** through the glasses, working from near distance first, and then moving toward the horizon, seeing absolutely nothing.

"Are you sure that's it?" Susanne asked. "I mean, for a sacred lake you expect something bigger."

The question irritated Leaphorn.

"Didn't Thomas Aquinas teach you white people that an infinite number of angels can dance on the head of a pin?"

"I don't think I heard about that," Susanne said. "I **cut out of** school in the tenth grade."

"Umm . . . well, the point is it doesn't take much water to cover a lot of spirits. But as far as *we're* concerned, it doesn't matter whether this is Kothluwalawa. What matters is whether George thinks it is. And *that* only matters if he came here and we can find him."

"I don't think he'd come here," she said doubtfully. "Why would he? Can you think of any reason?"

"All I know about George is what people tell me," Leaphorn said. "I hear he's sort of a mystic. I hear he's sort of crazy. I hear **he's unpredictable**. I hear he wants to become a member of the Zuñi tribe, that he wants to be initiated into their religion. O.K. Let's say some of that is true. Now, I *also* hear that

----

methodically slowly and carefully

cut out of quit; dropped out of

he's unpredictable you cannot guess what he will do next

Ernesto was his best friend. And that Ernesto was afraid he had broken a taboo by telling George more than you're supposed to tell **the uninitiated** about the Zuñi religion." Leaphorn paused, thinking about how it might have happened.

"Now. Let's say George left the bicycle where he was supposed to meet Ernesto and he wanders off somewhere. When he gets back, the bicycle is gone and so is Ernesto. That's natural enough. He thinks Ernesto didn't wait and he missed him. But he also notices that great puddle of blood. It would have been fresh then. It would have scared him. The next day he comes to school, looking for Ernesto. And he finds out Ernesto is missing. That's exactly the way it happened. Now, everybody tells me George is sort of crazy. Let's say he decides the kachinas have punished Ernesto for the broken taboo. George would have heard the legend about the boy who violated the secrecy rule and had his head cut off by the warrior kachinas. Maybe he wants to come here to ask the Council of the Gods to absolve him of any of the blame. Or maybe he came because here's where Ernesto's spirit will be coming to join the ancestors." Even as Leaphorn told it, it sounded unlikely.

"Remember," he said, "George asked you about whether the kachinas would absolve guilt. And remember he told Cecil he had to find the kachinas—that he had business with them."

"*Maybe* it's the way George would think," Susanne said. She glanced down at Leaphorn and then down at her hands. She pulled the cuff down over the scar. "**He was way out** in a

....

the uninitiated people who are not Zuñi

He was way out His thinking was very different from other people's thinking lot of ways. He and Ernesto were always talking about witches and werewolves and sorcery and having visions and that sort of thing. With Ernesto you could tell **it was mostly just talk**. But with George I think it was real."

"If he plans to be here when Ernesto's spirit arrives, we have a good chance of catching up with him. That would be sometime tomorrow. Maybe at dawn."

"What do you mean?"

"It takes five days' travel after death for the spirit to reach the Dance Hall of the Dead," Leaphorn said. "The Zuñis try to have the burial of one of their people within the same cycle of sun in which he died—so they had the funeral for Ernesto the same day they dug his body out from under that little landslide on the mesa. Had a quick funeral for him at the Catholic church and then after that the priests and the valuable men of his kiva held their graveside ceremonial. But in a way the funeral's not really over. They put five sets of fresh clothing in the **burial shroud** with the body. And on the fifth day he gets here—if this really is the place—and he passes the guarding spirits on the shore, and he joins the Council of the Gods and becomes a kachina."

"So you think George will be here tomorrow?"

Leaphorn laughed. "I don't know if I really think it, or whether I just can't think of any other possibility."

"Maybe he wants to be here to sort of say goodbye or something. I think Ernesto was the only friend he ever had. Maybe he wants to **make some sort of crazy gesture**."

....

it was mostly just talk he did not really believe it

burial shroud cloth used to wrap the body

make some sort of crazy gesture do something to show that Ernesto was special to him

"Like **suicide**?"

Susanne looked at Leaphorn with eyes too old for her face. "He might do something like that, I think. He wanted bad to be a Zuñi and I guess Ernesto was his only hope—if there ever was a hope. But it wasn't just that." Her teeth caught her lower lip, then released it. "He was so lonely. I think it must be bad to be a Navajo if being lonely bothers you."

The thought had never occurred to Leaphorn. He considered it, looking across the broken expanse of grass, brush, and erosion which faded away to empty blue distance across the pond. "Yeah," he said. "Like a mole that hates the dark."

"Were *you* thinking he might come here to kill himself? Or do Navajos do that?"

"Not much. Except with **the bottle**," Leaphorn said. "It's a little slower than a gun."

Around the lake Leaphorn found antelope tracks, some old moccasin imprints in the dried mud, and the various traces left by coyotes and porcupines and red fox—the **myriad** species of small mammals that standing water attracts in **arid** country. The moccasin marks pretty well eliminated any doubt that this playa had some religious significance even if it wasn't the Sacred Lake. Except for ritual events, Zuñis were no more likely to be wearing moccasins than were Navajos or FBI agents. But there were no signs of the hoofprints of George's horse, or of the boots that George would have been wearing. The only tracks of horses he found were old and almost erased, perhaps by the same windstorm that had howled around Shorty Bowlegs'

....

suicide killing himself
the bottle alcohol
myriad many
arid dry

hogan the night he was killed, and they didn't match the hoofprints Leaphorn had memorized there. Pastured horses, he guessed, watering here.

He worked his way away from the lake, searching in an expanding circle along game trails and sandy drainage bottoms. Susanne followed, asking a few questions at first, then falling silent. By 2 P.M. Leaphorn was absolutely certain that George Bowlegs hadn't come to this lake. He sat under a juniper, offered the girl a cigarette and smoked one himself, as he tried to imagine where else George might go to find his kachinas. There didn't seem to be an answer. He finished the cigarette and **resumed** the search. Within five minutes he found, clear and unmistakable, the shape of the left forefoot of George's horse. It was in the bare earth where the bulk of a rabbit bush shielded it from the wind. Leaphorn then found the right front hoofprint in the open, so wind-erased that he would have missed it if he hadn't known where to look.

"So he did come," Susanne said. "But where do we look for him now?"

"He was here either before or during that little storm," Leaphorn said. "It must have been still light. So he made part of the trip Monday night after he left the note for Cecil and then finished the ride Tuesday."

And then what? Leaphorn examined the ground around the bush, picking up traces of hoof tracks in places where the ground cover or **earth contour** had offered some protection from the blasting wind. The short distance he **scouted**

....

resumed continued

earth contour shape of the ground

scouted explored

suggested that George had ridden up this ridge from the northeast—the direction of Zuñi Village. The boy had sat his horse for a considerable time behind a growth of piñon, and then had ridden some thirty yards along the ridge and away toward the southeast. Southeast there was the gray-green shape of the Zuñi **escarpment**. He had found the lake and then he had ridden away. Why? To wait? To wait for what? For Cata's spirit to arrive tomorrow for its **descent** into the underworld? Maybe. Leaphorn shook his head. Susanne was looking at him doubtfully.

"You're sure about him not taking food from the commune?" he asked.

"I'm sure," she said. "Halsey wouldn't let him have any."

"So he must have been hungry by the time he got here. The boy's hungry and he's proud of his ability as a deer hunter, and he's brought along his deer rifle. So I'd guess he'd go deer hunting." Otherwise, if he was waiting for Cata's spirit, he would have had two full days to pass without any food. There were no deer tracks here. The herds would still be back on the **plateau,** not yet driven down to low ground by snow and cold. If George was smart he'd head for the plateau, find a place with shelter, and **hole up**. And then he would find a herd territory and set up over a deer trail, and have meat to eat while he waited for whatever he waited for.

And because George Bowlegs knew how to find deer, Leaphorn knew how to find Bowlegs. That left the question of what to do with this skinny girl. Leaphorn looked at her

---

escarpment cliffs
descent movement down
plateau raised, flat area of land
hole up hide

speculatively, and explained **the alternatives**. They were simple enough. She could find her way back to the truck and wait for him there—perhaps until sometime late tomorrow. Or she could come along, which would involve a substantial amount of long-distance walking, and maybe spending a cold night on the plateau. "I don't know if it's dangerous," Leaphorn said. "I don't think George killed the Cata boy, but some people think so, and if he did maybe he'd want to shoot me because I'm hunting him. I doubt it, but then, as I said, everybody says he's sort of crazy. If he is crazy enough to take a shot at somebody, all he's got is a worn-out short-range 30-30. But actually, if he's good enough to stalk deer with that thing, I wouldn't want him **stalking** me." He paused. Was there anything he'd **overlooked**? He had a feeling there might be. "Another thing. He's almost sure to see us before we see him. Because we'll have to be moving and he probably won't be."

Susanne was smiling at him. "On the other hand," she said, "George likes me and he trusts me and he isn't going to shoot at me. I don't think he's going to shoot at anybody else, either, and I'd rather come along than be at that truck all night by myself. And if I don't come along you'll never find him, because when he sees a strange man, he'll hide. But if he sees me, he'll come out and talk. I'd rather come along."

Leaphorn led the way down the ridge at a fast walk.

The route Bowlegs must have taken—the shortest and easiest way up the mesa—was a saddle-backed ridge which provided access up the mesa wall. He would track just long

....

speculatively questioningly

the alternatives what her choices were

stalking following

overlooked not considered

enough to confirm this and then head directly for the saddle. Susanne was hurrying along behind him.

"I'm kinda scared," she said. "I bet you are a little, too, aren't you? But I really *do* think George needs somebody to help him."

Exactly, Leaphorn thought. George, and Ted Isaacs, and the pale young man with nightmares, and a younger sister left somewhere back in cruel country, and a world full of losers—they all need Susanne's help, and they'll get it if she can reach them. Which is what keeps her from being a loser, too. He walked fast, **picking up** the wind-faded hoofprint here and there, knowing Susanne would **keep up**, and trying without any luck at all to understand the choice Ted Isaacs had made.

....

picking up finding
keep up be able to stay with him

BEFORE YOU MOVE ON...

1. **Character** Leaphorn returns to the Bowlegs's hogan for a third time. What does this show about Leaphorn?

2. **Generalization** Based on what you know about Leaphorn, what is the most important characteristic of a detective?

LOOK AHEAD Read pages 162–173 to find out if Leaphorn and Susanne find George.

15

Thursday, December 4, 2:17 P.M.

They found the tracks of George's horse on the saddleback slope, about where Leaphorn expected to find them.

"You're good at this, aren't you," Susanne said.

"I've been doing it a long time," Leaphorn said.

She was squatting on her heels at the deer trail beside him, inspecting the hoofprint. Her left hand continued to tug absently at her right cuff, pulling the frayed fabric over the scar. The reflex of a bruised spirit. How badly bruised? Leaphorn **set his mind to building a set of circumstances under which** this too-thin child-woman would have killed Ernesto Cata **in some schizophrenic perversion of good purpose**. His imagination managed that job, but failed at the next one— which attempted to place her in the Bowlegs hogan with a weapon raised over the head of a helpless drunk.

From the mesa top above them there came the raucous cry of a piñon jay. Leaphorn listened, heard nothing else. The breeze was dead now. Nothing moved. On the western horizon, somewhere over central Arizona, a grayish fringe of clouds had formed. Leaphorn wished he had listened to the weather

....

set his mind to building a set of circumstances under which tried to think about why

in some schizophrenic perversion of good purpose in a state of mental illness and confusion

162

forecast. He felt suddenly nervous. Had something startled the jay? Was George Bowlegs with his old 30-30 looking down at them from the rimrock? Had he guessed wrong about the boy? George couldn't have killed his father. He was a day's ride away from the hogan. But he could have killed Cata. Could he be not just a mixed-up way-out kid but literally insane? **Living some fantasy of sorcery-witchcraft unreality** that made murder just another part of the dream? The question occupied Leaphorn on the steep climb up the saddle over the lip of the mesa and caused him to move more slowly and cautiously as he went about his work. Even so, within an hour he had **accumulated** most of the information he needed.

In this season, this end of the mesa was the grazing territory for a herd of perhaps twenty to twenty-five mule deer. They watered at a seep under the rimrock and had two regular sleeping places—both on heavily brushed hummocks where updrafts would carry the scent of predators toward them. Within two hours he had a fair idea of the pattern the herd followed in its dawn, twilight, and **nocturnal** feedings. This feeding pattern, he explained to Susanne, was followed with almost machinelike rigidity by mule deer—varying only with changing weather conditions, wind, temperature, and food supplies.

"From what you tell me about George, he's going to know all this," Leaphorn said. "If he got up here when we think he did, he would have been trying to get one about dusk. He'd have done enough track reading to figure out where the deer

....

Living some fantasy of sorcery-witchcraft unreality Living in a fantasy of witches and magic

accumulated gathered

nocturnal nighttime

browsed when they came out of their afternoon sleeping place. Then he'd set up an ambush and just wait."

The ravens led them to the spot. The guard bird rose, cawing an alert. A dozen feeders flapped skyward in his wake, noisy with alarm. And down the slope they found the small clearing where George had shot his deer.

The animal, a small two-year-old buck, still lay beside the trail in the shadow of an outcropping of cap rock boulders. Leaphorn stood on one of the boulders surveying the scene and feeling good about it. For the first time since he had heard of George Bowlegs, **something seemed to be working out with that rational harmony** Leaphorn's orderly soul demanded. He explained it to Susanne, showing her the scuff marks on the lichens where George had crouched on the boulders; explaining how, at dusk, the cooling air would be moving down the trail, taking George's scent away from the approaching herd and allowing him to perch almost directly over their route.

"From here we pick up his tracks and find where he spent last night. He'll have the horse hobbled somewhere close, so that should be easy. And if he's marking time until tomorrow . . ." Leaphorn's voice trailed off. His expression, which had been blandly satisfied, deteriorated into a puzzled frown. He broke the self-created silence by muttering something in Navajo. A moment ago this scene had **clicked tidily into the framework his logic had built**—a deer killed where, when, and how the deer should have been killed. Why hadn't he seen the glaring incongruity? Leaphorn's frown **decayed into a glower**.

....

something seemed to be working out with that rational harmony things were making sense like

clicked tidily into the framework his logic had built made sense

decayed into a glower became an angry look

Susanne was looking at him, surprised. "What's the matter?"

"You wait right here," he said. "I want a closer look at this."

He swung himself down off the boulders and squatted beside the carcass. It was stiff, dead not much less than a day. The smell of fresh venison and old blood rose into his nostrils. It was a fat, young, four point buck, shot just behind the left shoulder from above and in front—a perfect shot for an instant kill and made, obviously, from the boulder at very short range. George had then rolled the buck on its back, removed the scent glands from its rear legs, tied off the anal vent, opened the chest cavity and the abdomen with a neat and precise **incision through hide** and muscles. He had rolled out the **entrails**, and then he had cut a long strip of hide and tied it to the buck's front ankles, presumably in preparation for **hoisting the carcass** from a tree limb to let it drain and cool away from ground rodents. But the carcass still lay there. Leaphorn scowled at it. He could have understood if George had simply sliced himself a substantial portion of venison and let the carcass lie. It would have gone against the grain, as Navajo and hunter, to waste the meat. But if he had been in a hurry George might have done it. Why this, though? Leaphorn rocked back on his heels and tried to re-create it.

The boy carefully scouting the herd without alerting it, checking its browsing routes, checking the wind drift, setting his ambush, waiting silently in the gathering darkness, picking the deer he wanted, firing the single precise shot in the proper

....

incision through hide cut through skin
entrails guts; inner organs
hoisting the carcass lifting the body

place. Then bleeding his kill, taking each step in **dressing** the carcass, without sign of hurry. And then, with the job almost done, walking away and leaving the meat to spoil without even cutting himself a steak to roast.

"What are you doing?" Susanne asked. "Is something wrong?"

"Look around there and see if you can find the **empty rifle shell**."

"What would it look like?"

"Brass," Leaphorn said. "Smaller than a fountain pen cap." He poked through the entrails. The heart was missing, and the liver, and the gall bladder. The ravens had been at work, but they wouldn't have had time to finish off the large organs and would have avoided the bitter gall. It was useful to a Navajo only for ceremonial purposes, for medicine, to **fend off** witches. Leaphorn tried to remember if the gall of deer had any ritual use for the Zuñis. Something about a hunting fetish, he thought, but he didn't know much about their ceremonialism. He confirmed that George had taken no meat. At one point an incision had been made and some fat cut out. Why would George want **tallow**? Leaphorn could think of no answer. And why kill a deer for meat, start a neat butchering job, and then walk away with nothing but heart and liver? They'd said George was crazy, but insanity wouldn't explain this.

Leaphorn rose from the crouch, noticing that his muscles were tired. He began with little hope or enthusiasm to determine what sort of story the tracks around this clearing

....

dressing preparing
empty rifle shell used bullet
fend off keep away
tallow fat

would tell.

Deer tracks were everywhere. Near the carcass their frantic hoofs had churned the trail. George had walked here. The sign of his boots was plain over the hoof marks.

So was the print of the moccasin.

Leaphorn stared at this track—a soft, medium-sized, foot-shaped impression. And then his hand was fumbling at the flap of his pistol holster as the implications of what he was seeing became clear. He stood motionless, his eyes scanning the brush which surrounded this small opening, his hand on the butt of the pistol. The footprint had been made yesterday—after George had killed his deer but not long afterward. Someone had followed George here. In some unmeasurable fraction of a second, mind and memory **fit pieces together**. Leaphorn saw Cecil's battered tin lunchbox with **keepsakes** disordered by a searching hand. He heard Cecil's voice saying that the note from George had been left in the box. In that instant Leaphorn knew what he had been overlooking for thirty-six hours. The note was missing from the box because the man who killed Shorty Bowlegs had found it, and from it had calculated where George had gone, and had relentlessly tracked him to this spot.

Leaphorn cursed himself vehemently in Navajo. How could he have been so stupid? This is what **his subconscious had been prodding him** to remember. Had he remembered it too late? He glanced at the carcass. This person must have arrived as George was **dressing** the deer, which explained why George had abandoned the job unfinished. So where was George now?

....

fit pieces together made sense of the clues
keepsakes possessions
his subconscious had been prodding him he had been trying
dressing butchering, taking organs out of

Had the man killed him and hidden the body?

"Here it is." Susanne's voice was behind him. "It's more like a lipstick than a fountain pen cap." She was holding up **an empty cartridge** between thumb and forefinger, grinning. (It wouldn't be an empty 30-30 from George's old rifle, Leaphorn thought. It would be .45 caliber, or .38, or 30-06, and it would proclaim that George Bowlegs had been shot to death at this spot yesterday about the same time Lieutenant Joseph Leaphorn had been wasting his time chatting with a Catholic priest in Zuñi.)

"Let's see it," Leaphorn said. Susanne dropped into his palm an empty 30-30 shell, its copper percussion cap dented, its mouth still smelling faintly of burned powder.

"It was right at the base of that big rock," Susanne said. "Was it from George's gun?"

"It was from George's rifle," Leaphorn said. "Now see if you can find another one. Look around the **fringes of this clearing** . . . around places where somebody could stand and look in here without being seen."

Susanne's face made a question. He didn't answer it. Instead he began the **tedious** job of finding how George had left this spot.

First he found the way George had arrived. He had come up the deer trail from below. It took another fifteen minutes to sort out the footprints and determine the way the boy had left. Leaphorn felt tremendous relief. George had left under his own power, walking directly away from the carcass and back around the boulder. There he had turned, crouched with his weight on

....

an empty cartridge a used bullet
fringes of this clearing edges of this area
tedious long and slow

the balls of his feet, facing back into the clearing. (Doing what? Listening? Watching? Had something alerted him?) From there the footprints led past a screen of piñons, past another stony outcrop, and up the slope into heavier timber.

Leaphorn spent another half hour at the clearing and learned little more. In her fruitless hunt for another empty cartridge (which Leaphorn no longer expected to find), Susanne startled a cottontail rabbit from his brush pile den beyond the clearing and sent him bolting through the rocks. That sort of sound might have been what had **alerted the boy**. Whatever it had been, the boy had been nervous enough to take a covered, indirect route to the place where he had left his horse. From there he had ridden westward across the mesa.

Leaphorn sat on the trunk of a fallen **ponderosa**, fished out his emergency can of potted meat from his jacket pocket, and divided it with Susanne. While they ate he considered alternatives. He could continue trying to follow George's tracks, or he could wait and try to catch him at the lake tomorrow, or he could give up and go home. The **odds** of finding George now that he had been frightened **looked dismal**. The boy would either be running (but not very fast, because his horse would be nearly dead by now from hunger and exhaustion) or he would be hiding somewhere, very alert and very cautious. If Leaphorn had guessed right about the lake, the chance of catching George there looked a little better. At least they were the best odds available.

The sun was low now. The clouds in the west had risen up

....

alerted the boy let the boy know there was danger
ponderosa pine tree
odds chances
looked dismal were not good

the horizon and were fringed with violent yellows. Slanting light was turning the alkali and calichi flats in the valley below from white and gray into rose and pink. Seventy miles southwestward, another cloud formation had formed over the dim blue shape of the White Mountains. This great vacant landscape reminded him of Susanne's remark about it being hard to be a Navajo if you minded being lonely. He wondered about George again. The boy's flight from the deer carcass seemed to suggest **taut nerves** more than panic. He had heard something, seen something, had been suddenly fearful, and had **ducked away**. He would hide somewhere safe, Leaphorn thought, rather than run wildly. And today his fears would have diminished with the light. George Bowlegs, Leaphorn decided, would still, right now, be on this mesa waiting for whatever he was waiting for at the Dance Hall of the Dead. But would the man who hunted him still be here? Leaphorn considered this. The man would have known he had **flushed his bird**. He needed to be **a fairly competent tracker** to find George's kill site. But once George was running, covering his tracks, he would have to be much better than that. He would have to be as good as Joe Leaphorn—and perhaps better than Leaphorn. As far as Leaphorn knew, there were no better trackers than himself. Certainly no Zuñi, or white man.

So what would the Man Who Wore Moccasins do? Leaphorn thought of the bloody head of Shorty Bowlegs, the ransacked hogan. He doubted if the man would give up. He would stay in a likely place with a long view and wait for

....

taut nerves nervousness

ducked away hid

flushed his bird made George run

a fairly competent tracker good at following things

the boy to make a move. Leaphorn looked toward Susanne, who was sprawled on her back, her face dusty and drawn with fatigue. Too tired to talk. He pushed himself to his feet, more tired himself than he'd been since as far back as he could remember.

"We've got a little bit of light left," he said. "I think we'll cut back toward that **saddle** where we climbed up here. That was George's way up and it's probably his way down. We'll find a place to get some rest somewhere near there. And in the morning we'll be in position to watch for him."

"You're not going to try to find him tonight?"

"I'm going to try to get some general idea of about where he might be," Leaphorn said. "And then we're going to rest."

On the **rimrock** above the saddle, Leaphorn stopped again. He got out his binoculars and spent five minutes examining the landscape. The saddle, as it had appeared from the lake, seemed to be the only easy way down. Beyond the saddle, south of the cliff on which Leaphorn stood, a shelf of land extended from the escarpment. The timber there was a thick jumble of mixed dry-country **conifers**. He had noticed it before, spotting it as ideal deer cover—the sort of place a deer herd would pick for a resting place. A single neck of land connected this great hill with the mesa. Against the rimrock, the deer could not be approached from above because of the overhung cliff. They could watch the backtrail, as resting deer always did, with no trouble. Rising air currents during the day would carry up to them the scent of any **predator**. And there were escape

....

saddle ridge; mountain pass
rimrock cliff
conifers trees
predator hunter

routes. The way down was steep but, unlike the mesa cliffs, not impossible. Leaphorn studied this site through the binoculars. It would be attractive to George for the same reason it would appeal to deer. It offered security without being a trap. George had seen it. He must have seen its advantages as a hiding place.

At the head of the saddle, they crossed the **game** trail which led down it. Susanne had revived slightly now. "There's our tracks," she said. "Your boots and my **tennies**. And there's George's horse's hoofprint that we saw going up."

"Yeah," Leaphorn said. If she was **reviving**, he wasn't.

"And here's one of those moccasin tracks," she said. "Like the one you showed me back at the deer."

"Where!"

"Right here. He stepped on your footprint."

Leaphorn squatted beside the track. The moccasin, going down the trail, had partially erased the heel mark Leaphorn had left that afternoon on the way up.

Susanne read something in his face. "Is that bad luck, or something? Someone stepping on your footprint?"

"I guess it depends," he said. He hadn't explained to her who must have left the prints at the carcass of the deer. There hadn't been any reason to frighten her. Now maybe he should tell her. The man who had been stalking George yesterday might now be stalking them. At least, he knew they were on the mesa. Leaphorn would decide what to tell her after they had found a place to spend the night.

By the time they reached the access route to the wooded

....

game animal
tennies tennis shoes; sneakers
reviving waking up; getting more energy

peninsula of land below the rimrock, the western sky was the violent red of dying sunset. Due east there was the faint yellow glow where soon the full moon would be rising. Leaphorn stood at a gap in the rimrock, looking down the inevitable game path which led away into the brush.

"If I had hurried a little," he said, "I could see something." No tracks were visible in the **dusk** on the narrow trail. George might have avoided it, anyway, if he suspected he was followed. Far away and behind them, Leaphorn heard a **yipping bark**. The calm cycle of day was ending. Now the hunting cycle began—the hours of the predator, the owl, and the bobcat, the coyote and the wolf. There was no breeze at all, only the faint movement of the **ground thermal**, cold air sifting past him, sinking toward the valley far below. He was suddenly nervously aware that the Man Who Wore Moccasins knew they were on this mesa. Had the man found them? Had he watched them? Was he watching them now? The thought made Leaphorn conscious of a spot of itching skin between his shoulder blades. He decided to tell Susanne about the moccasin tracks. He would do it while they were eating. She should know.

"Susie," he said. "Keep your eyes open. I'm going down here just a little ways and see if I can see anything."

He took, as it turned out, exactly three steps.

---

dusk setting sun

yipping bark coyote

ground thermal breeze near the ground

BEFORE YOU MOVE ON...

1. **Sequence** Reread page 169. What does Leaphorn think happened after George killed the deer?

2. **Conclusions** Reread page 172. Why is Leaphorn alarmed when Susanne sees the moccasin tracks?

LOOK AHEAD Read pages 174–188 to find out why Susanne must protect Leaphorn.

» 16 «

Thursday, December 4, 6:08 P.M.

The pain was like being struck by a hammer. Leaphorn staggered a step backward. He gasped for air, conscious simultaneously of the loud double crack of the shot, of the great knot of pain in his **abdomen**, of the stink of burned powder. Behind him he heard Susanne scream. His left hand had moved, without his willing it to move, to his stomach. His right hand fumbled under his jacket for the **pistol holstered** on his hip— an action equally reflex. His eyes had seen the source of this attack at the very moment it had happened. They had registered a jet of motion from the rocks directly ahead of him, and the streak of the **projectile** toward him. It seemed impossible that he could have seen the bullet. It seemed impossible that the shot had come from the very face of the rocks. His right hand held his pistol now, but there was no target. No one was there. No one could be there. And then he was conscious of what his left hand was feeling. It had found, projecting from his shirt just above his navel, a tube of metal. Leaphorn stared down at it, incredulous at first and then trying to understand what he was seeing.

....

abdomen stomach
pistol holstered gun he carried
projectile flying object

Projecting from his abdomen, the source of both the burned powder smell and his pain, was a cylinder of dull aluminum. A tangle of pink wool yarn was attached to its base. With a motion born of revulsion, Leaphorn jerked the cylinder away from his stomach. He flinched at the freshened pain. The cylinder was free from his flesh now, but caught on the tough khaki cloth of his shirt. He jerked it free. "What happened?" Susanne was shouting. "What's wrong?"

A steel **hypodermic needle**, half the diameter of a soda straw, jutted an inch from the front of the cylinder—red now with Leaphorn's blood. The cylinder was hot and stank of cordite. He stared at it without understanding. His finger found the barb which had caught in the cloth of his shirt. And then he knew what had stuck him. It was a hypodermic dart for stunning animals, used by zoos, game conservation officers, veterinarians, and animal biologists. He took six quick steps down the trail to the rocks. Carefully wedged into a **crevasse**, screened with dead leaves, was a black carbon dioxide pellet gun with a second tube attached to its top. A copper wire was tied to the **trigger mechanism**.

Susanne was beside him now, looking at the cylinder. "What is it?"

"**I tripped some sort of booby trap**," Leaphorn said. "And I got shot with this thing. It's what you shoot wild animals with when you want to capture them without killing them." Leaphorn unbuttoned his shirt and pulled apart the cloth enough to examine the wound. The puncture hole in the dark

....

hypodermic needle needle used for giving shots
crevasse deep crack
trigger mechanism gun's trigger
I tripped some sort of booby trap I set off a trap

skin looked, to Leaphorn, incredibly small. Only a little blood seeped from it. But what sort of **serum** had it blasted into his flesh? Thinking of that added a measure of panic to the knot of pain. He wasn't ready to think about it for another second or two. "The way it works, the cylinder is fired by a compressed gas—or, in some guns, by gunpowder. And when it strikes the animal, there's another little powder charge in the cylinder. That explodes and forces the serum down the needle into—into whatever you're shooting."

"The serum? What would it be?" Susanne's eyes were enormous. "What will it do to you?"

By now Leaphorn was asking himself the same question. "We'll guess it's the same stuff they shoot into animals. So we've got to hurry." He looked around him almost frantically. He ran down the path and then cut back toward the cliff.

"There," he said, pointing. "We'll get into that **depression** in the wall." He lost his footing twice scrambling up the mound of fallen stones under the rock wall of the mesa, and then sprawled onto the sand behind them. He inspected the site quickly. Given time he could have found something better, perhaps even a secure place to hide. Here whoever it was would find them, and it was too open from the front. But at least their rear and sides were protected. Nothing could reach them from above.

"What are—"

"Don't talk," Leaphorn said. "There isn't time." He handed her his pistol. "I'm going to be **out of it** in a minute, so listen.

....

serum drug
depression hole
out of it unconscious

176

Here's how this thing works." He showed her how to aim, how the revolver fired, the dozen spare cartridges in his belt, and how to reload. "Whoever set that trap either heard it fire or he's going to come around and check, and he'll know he got somebody and he'll find us. You're going to have to stay alert. When he comes, shoot him." He felt **a wave of nausea** and raised his hand to rub his forehead. It took a concentrated effort of will to control the hand. "Try to kill him," Leaphorn said. His voice sounded thick in his ears now, and fierce with rage. "If you don't keep him away, I think he'll kill us. I think he's crazy."

It was hard now to control his tongue. "This stuff is **paralyzing me**. I think it wears off in a few hours and I'll be all right again. Don't let me smother if I fall over, or swallow my tongue or anything. And if I die, try to **slip away** in the dark. Find the highway." Talking now was an immense effort. His legs were numb. He wanted to move his feet. The message left his brain, but nothing happened. "Don't get lost," he said. "Moon rises east, goes down west. Try . . ." His tongue would no longer rise from his teeth to form the sound.

When he could no longer talk, when he could do nothing, panic arrived . . . a frantic dream of **suffocation**, of drowning helplessly in his own fluids. He fought it down grimly, controlling his mind, as he could no longer control his body. The panic left as quickly as it had come. Left him calm, studying the effects of the drug. It seemed now to have included an almost total paralysis of all voluntary muscles

....

a wave of nausea sick to his stomach
paralyzing me making me unable to move
slip away escape
suffocation not being able to breathe

without affecting involuntary actions—the blink of the eyes, **the rhythmic expansion-contraction of the lungs**. Leaphorn considered all this **with an odd sort of detachment**. He tried to remember what he had heard about this method of stunning animals. Paralytic drugs must block passage of the message from brain to muscle. Otherwise, if all muscles were paralyzed, breathing would cease. His mind still seemed clear—unusually clear, in fact—and his hearing was excellent. He simply could not move. It was as if his brain had been partly disconnected from his body—still receiving the sensory inputs of eyes and ears and nerve endings, but unable to react with commands to action.

How long would the paralysis last? He remembered a wildlife film he had seen on television—a rhino shot with such a dart for study by a biologist. What had they said about it? Several hours, he thought. How many is several? How would it affect a man? And what sort of drug had been used? No profit in speculation. He turned to other thoughts, impressed with how clearly his mind was working. Impressed, too, with how immense the rising moon looked emerging over the eastern horizon. Susanne had stopped trying to talk to him, recognizing that he could not respond. She sat beside him, her back to the dark. Where had the man got the rig? It would be easy enough, Leaphorn guessed. Veterinary-supply houses would have the dart guns and the serums. Maybe the drug would require **a prescription**. Leaphorn guessed that if it did, just about any rancher or game ranger or zoologist could

....

the rhythmic expansion-contraction of the lungs breathing
with an odd sort of detachment without emotion
a prescription an order from a doctor for medicine

manage to get the stuff.

He noticed, with mild surprise, that he could hear Susanne breathing. Faintly rasping intake, sighing exhalation. He could hear incredibly well. Somewhere on the cliff above, a night bird was moving. At some immense distance on the mesa a coyote yipped twice and then sang its warbling song. And somewhere to his front, somewhere behind the screen of rabbit brush and juniper on this rocky hill, there were the footsteps of a human. They were slow footsteps, carefully placed—the footsteps of a hunter stalking. Leaphorn found himself wishing almost casually that he could force his tongue to tell Susanne about this danger. At another level of consciousness he wondered about this lack of fear, this immense gain in ability to hear, and this odd feeling of detachment. He remembered a similar sensation from years ago at Arizona State when he and Tom Bob and Blackie Bisti and another Indian student had gone to a meeting of the Native American Church and he had sampled the bitterness of a ceremonial peyote button. He noticed that he could remember this incident with exact and detailed clarity. He was in the smoky room, **acrid with some unfamiliar incense**, seeing the sweat darkening the back of Blackie's shirt, everything. The stuffiness of rebreathed air, the drone of words, the grim face of the Kiowa preacher giving them their instructions. He listened to the **sermon** again, thinking now as he had then that it contained an odd mixture of Christianity, mysticism, and Pan-Indian nationalism. And now, as then, Leaphorn was quickly bored with it. And he left the smoky

....

acrid with some unfamiliar incense with a strange, bad smell

sermon religious speech

room, drifting out through time and space, and was again under the moon, which was approaching now, so close, so large, that its dark yellow form filled his entire skull with cold. He could no longer see around it. There was only moon in his field of vision, an immense disk of ice pulsing in the black sky. And then Susanne was speaking to him. Her whisper **thundered around his head**, the words indescribably slow. "Mr. Leaphorn, can you hear me? I think there is something out there. I think I hear something. Mr. Leaphorn! *Mr. Leaphorn!*" Her hand was on his chest, her face close to his, her hair blotting out the yellow disk, fear in her eyes, her face almost **frantic**. And more words. "Mr. Leaphorn. Please don't die." I won't, Leaphorn thought. I will never die.

But perhaps he would die. He could hear the footsteps of the hunter clearly. The hunter now stood behind the tangle of chamiso and juniper which the moonlight had turned from gray to silver. Now the hunter moved again, closer. He stopped behind the juniper with the broken limb. There now in the darkness diluted by the moonlight was the face of whatever it was that made these creaking footfalls. Obviously it was a bird. Perhaps a bird extinct since Folsom Man had hunted here. It was much larger than any physical bird, odd and angry. Its eyes stared, round and blank and dead, from a face that was black and yellow and blue, but mostly black. The eye sockets were empty, he saw. The bird's skull was hollow. And being hollow must be dead. Yet it moved. The **rampant plume of feathers at its summit** bristled with movement and its rigid beak angled

....

thundered around his head was very loud

frantic wildly excited from fear

rampant plume of feathers at its summit big group of feathers on the top of its head

outward past a juniper limb, reflecting the moonlight.

Beside him Susanne sucked in her breath and made a strangled sound. Leaphorn's pistol rose in her hand. It shattered the moon with a great flash of light and blast of sound. Now there was the smell of exploded powder. The echo rolled away around the mesa walls. Boom. Boom. Boom. Boom. Finally it **melded** into the other night sounds and faded away. The bird was gone now. Leaphorn could hear only the sound of crying. His hand fell from his leg and crashed into the ground. Leaphorn willed for a moment that it would rise again and **restore itself to its perch** away from the stony ground. But the hand simply lay there and Leaphorn retreated from it, and lost himself, falling, falling, falling into a glittering psychedelic dream in which the cold moon again pulsed in **an inky void** and a hunter sat naked on a ridge, working with infinite patience, chipping out lance points from pink ice, breaking them, dropping the broken parts onto the earth beside him, taking defeat after defeat without a show of anger.

Much later he became aware that Susanne had again fired the pistol. There was a thunder of sound all around him which forced the moon back into the sky. He was cold. Freezing, he thought. His hands were freezing. He managed some sort of sound, something between a sigh and a grunt. "You're all right," Susanne's voice whispered at his ear. "Your breathing sounds good, and your pulse seems O.K., and I think everything is going to be all right." She picked up his hand, turned it, looked at his wristwatch. "It's been almost four hours now, so maybe

....

melded blended
restore itself to its perch return to his leg
an inky void a dark sky

that stuff won't be working much longer." She stared into his face. "You can hear me, can't you? I can tell. You're getting awful cold. Your hands are like ice. I'm going to build a fire."

He focused **every molecule of his will** on an effort to say "No." He **managed only a grunt**. The psychedelic dream was gone for the moment and his mind was clear of **hallucinations**. She shouldn't build the fire. The Man Who Wore Moccasins might still be out there, waiting. By firelight, he might have light enough to shoot them. Again he managed a grunt, but the effort exhausted him. Susanne was away in the darkness. He could hear her moving. Gathering sticks. The moon had moved now, climbing up the sky and edging southward far enough behind the rim of the mesa so that the shadow extended ten yards beyond his feet. Outside the shadow, the landscape glittered gray and silver with moonlight. Nothing moved. His hearing still seemed to be unusually **acute**. From far, far away he heard the song of the coyote again, so dim by distance that it seemed to drift down from the stars. And then there was the sound, from much closer, of a hunting owl. The grotesque bird he had seen in his hallucination, the bird that had vanished after Susanne fired at it, must have been a kachina mask. Leaphorn thought about it. He recognized the mask. The bristling black ruff around the neck, the fierce plume of eagle feathers atop the head, the long tubular beak.

He had seen the mask before, in the moonlight behind the hogan at Jason's Fleece, and painted in the mural in the Zuñi mission. It was the Salamobia, the warrior who carried a

....

every molecule of his will all his energy
managed only a grunt only made a small sound
hallucinations imaginary visions
acute good

whiplike sword of tight-woven yucca. He tried to summon from his memory what he knew of this kachina. There were two of them at Shalako ceremonials, dancing attendance on the other members of the Council of the Gods. But each of the six Zuñi kivas was represented by one—so the total must be six. So six such masks must exist. And each would be carefully guarded by the Zuñi who had been chosen by his kiva for the honor of personifying this figure. The mask would be kept in its own room, provided with food and water, and the spirit which **resided** within it honored by prayer.

Susanne was lighting the fire now. Having accepted that it was impossible to warn her, Leaphorn ignored this. What would be, would be. He would enjoy being warm again. Now, while he could, he would think. But no more of the mask. The **genuine** masks would be guarded, but anyone could make a **counterfeit**.

The flame spread through the pile of leaves and twigs, crackling, casting a flickering yellow light. The dart had been **intended** for George. Apparently not meant to kill him. At least not immediately. Why not? Was it because this person—like Leaphorn—wanted to talk to the boy?

And why had George taken the gall from the deer? Dried, it would be useful as medicine, for use in curing ceremonials. And why take the fat from under the deerskin? There was something Leaphorn should remember about that. Something to do with Zuñi hunting procedures. He had heard about it from his roommate. He and Rounder had compared Navajo and Zuñi origin myths, emergence myths, migration myths,

....

resided lived

genuine real

counterfeit fake mask

intended meant

methods of doing things. Part of it, he remembered, concerned hunting.

The Navajo myth cautions against killing any of the sixty or so beings which had joined the First People in their escape from the Fourth World to Earth Surface World, which limited hunting **pretty well** to deer, antelope, and a few game birds. The Zuñi legend told of the great war against Chakwena, the Keeper of the Game, which was won only after the Sun Father created the two Zuñi War Gods to lead them. There had been beer and talk far into the night. He forced his mind to recall it. Rounder, his moon face bland, telling them how Father Coyote had taught Clumsy Boy the prayers that would persuade the deer that the hunter brought not harm, but **evolution into a higher being**. The fire flared up through the dry wood and Leaphorn felt the heat against his face. He felt, again, that odd sense of being detached from himself. He was slipping into another hallucinogenic nightmare. The sound of the fire became a **clamorous** rattle and crackle. The stars were brighter than they should be on such a night of moon. Yikaisdahi, the Milky Way, the billion bright footprints left by spirits on their pathway across the sky, glittered against the night. Leaphorn forced himself to concentrate. He could see Rounder, slightly drunk, his two hands framing the beer mug on the table, his face earnest, chanting it in Zuñi, and then the translation:

> *"Deer, Deer.*
> *I come following your hoofprints.*

....

pretty well mostly
evolution into a higher being change to something better
clamorous noisy

Sacred favors I bring as I run.
Yes, yes, yes, yes."

And then showing them, using the beer mug as the muzzle of the deer, how the Zuñi hunter breathed in the animal's last breath. And the prayer. How had it gone? Leaphorn remembered only that it was a statement of thanks that went with the drinking of the Sacred Wind of Life. And then the details of how the deer must be dressed, and of the making of the ball of deer fat and gall and blood from the heart and hair from the proper places, and some fetish offerings to be buried when the deer had fallen.

Suddenly Leaphorn could hear Rounder's drunken voice. "Don't eat in the morning. The hungry hunter scents game against the wind." And he was seeing Rounder's **placid** face against the sky just above the brightness of So'tsoh—the North Star—between the **constellations** Ursa Major and Cassiopeia, which the Navajos called Cold Man of the North and his wife. Then the nightmare was on him again, worse than before. The sky filled with the chindi of the dead. They wore deerskin masks and their great beaks clacked. He saw Slayer of the Enemy Gods, standing on a rainbow bright against the sky, but above him towered something with a great blue face and a tall white forehead, its chest covered with prayer plumes, holding a great wand edged with **obsidian**. Leaphorn knew somehow that this was Uyuyewi, the Zuñi War God, and he felt a hopeless dread. Then there was a face against his, breathing

....

placid peaceful
constellations groups of stars that formed
obsidian shiny, black rock

his breath, taking the wind of his life as it left his nostrils. And next, the hand of Susanne on his face, her voice in his ear. "Mr. Leaphorn. It's all right. It's going to be good again. Don't be afraid."

There was cold gray light against the eastern horizon now. And the fire was nothing but hot embers, and Leaphorn's mind told his shoulder muscles to huddle against the cold. And they did huddle, and his hand, told to rub his icy shoulder, rubbed it. Leaphorn was suddenly wide awake, the hallucinations a memory. Susanne was curled by the fire, asleep, the pistol by her hand. Leaphorn tried his legs. They, too, moved to command. He felt a fierce joy. He was alive. He was **sane**. He tried to push himself to his feet. Made it. Staggered for two steps, and then fell against the stone cliff with a clatter. He could control some muscles well, others not so well. The noise awoke Susanne.

"Hey, you're O.K." She had dead leaves in her hair, dirt on her face. She looked absolutely **exhausted** and tremendously **relieved**.

$$\rhd\lhd$$

It wasn't until after sunrise that Leaphorn had full control of all his muscles. His stomach bore a swollen red bruise where the dart had struck and fired its charge. He felt weak and sick. He suspected that would go away. He had planned to head for the lake, to try to reach it by sunrise—the sunrise of the fifth

....

sane not crazy

exhausted tired

relieved happy he was okay

day, when Ernesto Cata's spirit would arrive to join the Council of the Gods. But while he could walk a little, he couldn't walk straight. So instead they had waited by the saddle on the slight chance that George Bowlegs had not been frightened by the sound of pistol shots during the night and would be passing by. George did not appear. Leaphorn exercised as quietly as he could, concentrated on regaining full use of his legs. And he thought about **a diversity of** things. About what Ernesto Cata had told Father Ingles, about the odd way in which George Bowlegs had behaved, about Zuñi hunting ritual, about Ted Isaacs' speculation on how a Stone Age hunter had made his lance points, and about Halsey and the pale young man named Otis whose psychedelic nightmares Leaphorn could now better appreciate. He thought about why whoever had set the trap for George Bowlegs had used a hypodermic gun instead of a shotgun, and of other matters. And when, finally, **his right ankle would respond exactly as ordered**, he told Susanne they would return to the deer carcass and then head back for the truck.

"We'll cut off enough venison for some breakfast," Leaphorn said.

They did that. And after he had made a fire on which to roast it, he examined the ground around the carcass. He found a place where a small hole had been cut into the earth beside the carcass. Buried in it was a still softball of clay, blood, **tallow, gall**, and deer hair, the fetish offering Rounder had described for the fallen animal. Leaphorn carried it back to the fire, sat

....

a diversity of many different

his right ankle would respond exactly as ordered he could move his right ankle

tallow, gall fat and tissue

on the boulder, and pulled it apart carefully. Inside the ball he found a turquoise bead, the broken tip of a stone lance point, and a small bit of abalone shell.

BEFORE YOU MOVE ON...

1. **Cause and Effect** Reread pages 174–175. What causes Leaphorn to collapse?

2. **Inference** Reread page 205. Why is the fetish with the stone lance point that Leaphorn finds so important?

LOOK AHEAD Read pages 189–201 to find out who O'Malley suspects is the killer.

≫ **17** ≪

Friday, December 5, 2 P.M.

John O'Malley **made a tent out of his hands and looked** past Leaphorn at something at the back of the Zuñi Tribal Courtroom. "To sum it up," he said, "we still don't know where to **put our hands on** George Bowlegs."

He shifted his eyes slightly to look at Leaphorn. He smiled. The action made a dimple in each cheek and crinkled the skin around his blue eyes. "I hope you'll **stick to that chore**. I'd put somebody on it to work with you if there was anybody. But everybody is working on something else. I think that kid knows something about why Cata and Shorty Bowlegs were killed. And I think he can tell us something about that commune." The eyes shifted away and the smile turned off. "We really wanted to talk to him today."

Leaphorn said absolutely nothing.

"Second, you think somebody else is hunting George. Maybe so," O'Malley said. "I don't doubt it. I can see why maybe some people would want to shut him up. But it looks like he's hard to catch." The smile came on again. "And it's too bad you getting shot by that coyote trap or whatever it was. We'll

....

made a tent out of his hands and looked made a triangle with his thumbs and fingers and looked through it

put our hands on find

stick to that chore keep trying to find George

keep that syringe. Maybe we can track down where it came from and who bought the serum." The smile turned into a grin. "However, I think there's going to be enough **charges to file when we get this broken** so we may not need to worry about making a case on whoever committed that particular assault."

O'Malley folded the finger tent. The grin went away. He stood up.

"It might help," Leaphorn said quickly, "if you'd fill me in on what you've been learning."

O'Malley peered at him curiously.

"I gathered someone recognized Baker as a narcotics agent," O'Malley said. "He is." The silence stretched. That was all. Leaphorn realized with incredulous anger that this was all O'Malley was going to tell him.

"O.K. Then you think the commune is a cover for a narcotics drop—heroin or what have you," Leaphorn said. "And the killings were done to protect it?"

O'Malley said nothing.

"Is that right?" Leaphorn insisted.

O'Malley hesitated. Finally he said, "It's pretty obvious. But we haven't gotten everything we need yet to **get the indictments**. We need to talk to George. Among other things."

"Can I guess that Baker was working on this before the killings? That you've got enough so you don't have any doubts about it?"

O'Malley grinned again. "I'd say you could guess that."

"What have you got?"

....

charges to file when we get this broken crimes to accuse someone of committing

get the indictments accuse anyone of a crime

The grin faded. "For a long time," O'Malley said, "our policy has been that every officer working a case is told everything he needs to know about the part he is working on. But we don't **fill everybody in on everything that comes up** if it doesn't have anything to do with the **angle they're on**. For example, I can tell you that we'd really like to talk to George today—but I don't guess that's likely?"

"Why today?"

"Tomorrow's this big Zuñi Shalako ceremonial. Thousands of people here—strangers from all over. It would be a good cover for somebody to come in and make a pickup."

"Anybody in particular?"

There was another pause while O'Malley thought about it. He unzipped the briefcase on his desk and pulled out a sheaf of photographs. Some were official **police mug shots**. Some were candid shots of the sort stakeouts collect through telescopic lenses. Leaphorn recognized Halsey in a photograph that seemed to have been taken on a college campus, and the pale boy called Otis in a police mug photo. There were five others he didn't recognize, including a balding fat man and a young man with an Indian face in a paratroop uniform. Leaphorn picked up this photograph and examined it.

"If you see any of these birds around tomorrow, I want to know about it," O'Malley said.

"This guy a Zuñi?"

"Yeah. He got the habit in Vietnam and he's been involved in dealing some since he got back."

....

fill everybody in on everything that comes up tell all the police everything that we have learned

angle they're on part of the investigation they are working on

police mug shots pictures taken when someone is arrested

Leaphorn put the photograph on the desk.

"That's the motive for the killings then?" he said. "Keeping a narcotics operation **covered up**? You got enough to be sure of that?"

"That's right," O'Malley said. "We're sure."

"O.K.," Leaphorn said. "So I'll just **stick to finding** George for you."

Pasquaanti wasn't in his office but his secretary—a small, cheerful girl with a very round face and a striking display of squash blossom jewelry—sent someone to find him after being persuaded it was important. Pasquaanti listened **impassively** while Leaphorn told him about seeing the kachina at the commune, about the ambition of George Bowlegs to become a Zuñi, about the note the boy had left for his brother, and about what had happened on the mesa. The Zuñi interrupted only once. He asked Leaphorn to describe the mask.

"It had a thick ruff of feathers around the neck," Leaphorn said. "Black. Probably crow or raven feathers. Had a beak maybe six inches long and round, like a broom handle. And the mask was rounded on top, with a sort of wand of feathers pointing quills-forward as a topknot. Then there was a design drawn on the cheek. I think it was a Salamobia mask."

"There are six of those," Pasquaanti said. He took out his fountain pen and made a quick sketch on notepaper. "Like this?"

"Yes. That's it."

"What color was the face?"

----

covered up a secret
stick to finding continue to look for
impassively without much interest

"The face? It was black."

Pasquaanti looked old. Leaphorn hadn't noticed that before. "Mr. Leaphorn," he said. "I thank you for telling me this."

"Is there anything you can tell me?'

Pasquaanti thought about it. "I can tell you that the Salamobia you saw was not genuine. Black is the color of the Hekiapawa kiva, the Mole kiva. That mask is safe. It is always safe. So are the other masks. You can be sure of that."

"Then could someone have taken another mask?"

"There are two kinds of masks," Pasquaanti said. "Some are the actual kachina and the kachina spirit lives in them and they are fed and watered and taken care of with prayer plumes and everything they want. They are . . ." He paused, searching his English vocabulary for the right words. "Sacred," he said. "Very holy." He shook his head. Neither phrase was exactly right. "The other kind of mask is different. They are borrowed, and repainted to be used for different kachinas, and the spirit is not there."

"So perhaps someone might have taken one of those and changed it to look like a Salamobia?"

Pasquaanti considered this. His fingers folded and unfolded on the desk. "There are the bad among us," he said finally. "Some of us drink, and have learned the whiteman's greed, and aren't worth anything. But I don't think a Zuñi would take the mask of his family and use it like this."

The two men looked at each other silently. What Leaphorn described had been a **hideous desecration**. Worse, it had

---

hideous desecration terrible violation

happened in the most holy period of the Zuñi **liturgical** year—in the days of sacred retreat just before Shalako. If this ceremonial was not properly done, rain did not fall, crops did not sprout, and sickness and bad luck were **loosened** across the land.

"One more thing," Leaphorn said. "I think George Bowlegs is wild to become a Zuñi. Maybe that's not possible, but he thinks it is. I think he went to your sacred lake because he wanted to talk to your Council of the Gods. And from what he told his little brother, I think he will come to Shalako and maybe he will do something. I think it would be good if your people watched for him."

"We will."

"And the man who wore the mask. He was smart enough to figure out where to look for George. He will be smart enough to figure it out again."

"We will watch for that man," Pasquaanti said. His voice was grim. It caused Leaphorn to remember something that Rounder had told him years ago: in Zuñi mythology, the **penalty for sacrilege** is death.

....

liturgical religious

loosened set free

penalty for sacrilege punishment for a religious crime

≫ **18** ≪

Lieutenant Joseph Leaphorn spent the afternoon on the ridge that overlooks the village of Zuñi from the south. He had picked the place carefully. It was a relatively comfortable spot, with soft earth under his buttocks and a sandstone slab for a backrest. A growth of chamiso and a gnarled piñon made it unlikely that anyone would see him and wonder what the devil he was doing there. And the view was ideal for his purpose. To his left his binoculars covered the old wagon trail that wandered up the Zuñi Wash from the southwest. To his right he looked down on a newly graded reservation road that angled under Greasy Hill at the edge of the village, swerved past the Zuñi cemetery, and ran southward. One or the other of these two roads would provide the most direct route from the mesa where George Bowlegs had killed his deer to the Shalako ceremonials in Zuñi Village. There were countless other ways Bowlegs might come—if come he did—including leaving his horse, walking to the paved highway, and hitchhiking. But Leaphorn could think of no other activity that offered better odds than did sitting here. And **intercepting** Bowlegs was only one of the

....

intercepting catching

reasons he was here. There was also the chance it offered him to think. He had a lot of thinking to do.

The swollen bruise on his abdomen reminded him of the first puzzle. Why had the trap been set to catch George Bowlegs but not to kill him? Cata and Shorty Bowlegs had been cut down without qualm or hesitation. Why not George?

Leaphorn leaned back against the rock, squirmed into an easier position. Above him the sky was turning gray. The overcast had been building since noon. First it was nothing more than high-altitude humidity—a thin layer of stratospheric ice crystals which hung a glittering halo around the sun. Then a **semiopaque** grayness had crept in from north-northwest and the day gradually lost its light.

Why not George? Leaphorn felt the faintest trace of breeze on his cheek. Cold. It had been dead calm. The orgy of baking which caught up the women of Zuñi each Shalako season had reached its **climax** during the morning. Now most of the outdoor ovens were cooling. But a thin layer of blue smoke still hung in the air over the pueblo. It made a faint smear as far northwest as the Zuñi Buttes and eastward to the gaudy water tower at Black Rock. Even here, high over the valley and a half mile away, **Leaphorn's nose caught the vague scent of** baking bread and the perfume of burned piñon resin.

Already the wide shoulders of state road 53 were cluttered with cars and campers and pickups. The Zuñi people had come home from wherever they had wandered—college campuses, jobs in California and Washington. Those who called

....

semiopaque partially clear

climax highest point

Leaphorn's nose caught the vague scent of Leaphorn smelled

themselves the Flesh of the Flesh were drawn back to their birthplace for this great Coming Home of their ancestor spirits.

And with them came the curious, the tourists, **dilettante Indian lovers**, anthropologists, students, hippies, other Indians. Among the crowd would be the Zuñis' Brothers of the Pueblos: people from Acoma, Laguna, Zia, Hopi, Isleta, Santo Domingo, men who were priests of their own kivas, themselves **connoisseurs of** the metaphysics of nature, men with their own Dancing Gods who came to share in the ancient magic of their cousins. And, of course, the Navajos. In from the lonely hogans, with wives and children. Taller, rawboned, wearing their Levi's—looking on with a mixture of awe for great medicine made by these Callers of the Clouds, and the countryman's contempt for the dweller of towns.

Leaphorn sighed. Normally Zuñi Village held perhaps 3,500 of the 4,500 Zuñis. Tonight seven or eight thousand people would be crowded here. It would be, as O'Malley had said, the one time a stranger come to pay money or collect heroin would be least likely to be noticed. Leaphorn's anger at O'Malley had gone now, the victim of Leaphorn's habit of relating actions to causes. O'Malley would not be an agent of the FBI if **his mind did not operate in a manner which conformed to FBI standards**. Obviously someone in the agency had been interested in Halsey, or in Halsey's commune, before the killings. That would color O'Malley's thinking. And if O'Malley had no respect for Leaphorn as a policeman, Leaphorn must admit, in fairness, that he had no respect for

....

dilettante Indian lovers people interested in Native American culture

connoisseurs of experts in

his mind did not operate in a manner which conformed to FBI standards he did not think like FBI

O'Malley. He would think of other things. Why hadn't a shotgun been rigged into that trap set for Bowlegs? Or why hadn't the syringe been loaded with **cyanide**? Leaphorn considered the question, found no way to reach a conclusion, and skipped back to the beginning—back to Monday, when he had first arrived at Pasquaanti's office. From there he worked forward, examining each of the oddities that puzzled him.

There was a stir of activity in the village now—people gathering on the street that fronted along Zuñi Wash on the Old Village side. Leaphorn watched. Through his powerful navy-surplus binoculars he saw the figure of a boy, naked except for loincloth, crossing the footbridge behind a man in white buckskin. The boy wore a hood surmounted by a single feather. Mask and body were black, spotted with dots of red, blue, yellow, and white. The Little Fire God, Leaphorn knew— Shulawitsi entering the Old Village to make his ceremonial inspection of the sacred place before the entry of the Council of the Gods. Ernesto Cata was dead but the Little Fire God lived. The Badger Clan had provided another of its sons to personify this eternal spirit.

The afternoon **wore on**. Leaphorn watched the roads and pursued his thoughts. More activity in the village now. The sound of drums and flutes **barely audible** on the cold air. This would be the arrival of the Council of the Gods. They came dancing down Greasy Hill, past the white-painted village water tank. Some he could see through the magnifying lenses. The Fire God with a smoking cedar branch. Then Saiyatasha, the

....

cyanide a deadly poison
wore on continued
barely audible that could barely be heard

198

Rain God of the North, called Longhorn because of the great curved horn which jutted from the right side of his black-and-white mask. He was a **burly** man in white deerskin shirt and a blue-and-white kirtle, a bow in one hand and a deer-bone rattle in the other. And behind him Hu-tu-tu, who brought the rains from the south, his mask lacking the great horn. With Hu-tu-tu, the two Yamuhaktos, their round eye and mouth holes giving their masks an expression of silly, childlike surprise. And dancing attendance, two Salamobias—the same fierce beaked faces that Leaphorn remembered from his nightmare. In each hand they carried a heavy pointed whip wand of yucca blades. The crowd kept a respectful distance.

The procession disappeared into the village. The sun was lost now as the cloud cover steadily thickened. It was growing much colder. Below, two station wagons and a pickup truck pulled off the cemetery road and disgorged more than a dozen men and a load of **paraphernalia**. Several wore ceremonial kirtles and skullcaps of white doeskin. They would be the personifiers of the Shalako and their attendants. The group vanished beneath the slope.

Leaphorn reached into his pocket and extracted the turquoise bead, the abalone shell, and the broken flint lance tip. All were items to which both Navajo and Zuñi would **attach ritual significance**. Changing Woman had taught the Navajos the use of the gemstone and the shell in their curing ceremonies. They were appropriate fetish items for George to have offered to the spirit of the deer. And so was the flint tip.

....

burly big

paraphernalia items for the ceremony

attach ritual significance use in rituals

Leaphorn wasn't sure how the Zuñis valued such relics from older cultures, but Navajos rated anything used by the Old People as potent medicine. As a boy, he used to hunt for these relics. He'd find them turned up amid the gravel in arroyo bottoms, uncovered on hillsides when the Male Rain pounded away the centuries of dust, and exposed among the clumps of buffalo grass when the Wind People carved potholes in the dry earth. He would give them to his grandfather and his grandfather would teach him another song from the Night Way, or a story of the Holy Ones. Perhaps George had found this lance point in like manner. Or perhaps he and Cata had stolen it from the dig site and it had—despite the certainty of Reynolds and Isaacs—somehow not been missed. That seemed unlikely, however. It was too fine a sample of Stone Age workmanship. Or perhaps . . .

The fragment of flint in Leaphorn's palm became a sort of keystone. Around it the pieces of the puzzle of why Ernesto Cata had to die **fell exactly into place**. Suddenly Leaphorn knew why the trap set for George Bowlegs had not been a lethal trap, and what had happened in the hogan of Shorty Bowlegs, and why what George Bowlegs had told his brother about petty theft had been contradicted by Reynolds and Isaacs. He sat stock-still, sorting it very precisely in chronological order, checking for flaws, **assigning to each of those deeds which had seemed so irrational a logical cause**. He knew now why two murders had been committed. And he knew he couldn't prove it—could probably never prove it.

....

fell exactly into place began to make sense

assigning to each of those deeds which had seemed so irrational a logical cause finding logical answers to all the things that did not make sense

From below the hill came the noise of drum and rattle and a hooting sound. The Shalako emerged—the couriers of the Zuñi gods. The six huge ceremonial attendants. Leaphorn had forgotten how large they were. Ten feet tall, he guessed, to the ray of eagle feathers cresting their birdlike heads, so tall that the human legs supporting them under the great hooped skirts seemed **grotesquely out of proportion**. These immense birds would cross Zuñi Wash at sundown and be **escorted** to the houses that had been prepared for them. The sacred dancing and ceremonial feasting would continue until the following afternoon.

Leaphorn pushed himself to his feet, brushed the sand from his uniform, and began walking down the slope toward Zuñi Village. In that dim margin between day and night, the snow had begun. Heavy, wet, life-giving snow. Once again the Shalako had called the clouds and brought the water blessing to their people. One corner of Leaphorn's mind appreciated the harmony of this. Another urged him to hurry. Yesterday the killer had needed George Bowlegs alive. But if George Bowlegs came to Shalako, George Bowlegs would have to die.

....

grotesquely out of proportion too small for the Shalako

escorted led

BEFORE YOU MOVE ON...

1. **Character's Point of View** What does O'Malley think caused the deaths? Do you think Leaphorn agrees? Why?

2. **Conclusions** Reread pages 193–194. Why do you think someone is pretending to be a kachina?

LOOK AHEAD Read pages 202–220 to find out if Leaphorn finds the real killer.

>> **19** <<

Sunday, December 7, 2:07 A.M.

By 1 A.M., Leaphorn had decided he wasn't likely to find George Bowlegs. He had prowled the village tirelessly, elbowing his way through the crowds jamming each of the ceremonial houses, watching, and studying faces. The very nature of the ritual magnified the difficulty. By tradition, not more than two of the Shalako could be entertained in a single house. Separate houses had to be prepared for Saiyatasha and his Council of the Gods, and for the ten Koyemshi, the sacred clowns. Three of these houses were in the oldest part of the village, on the crowded hill overlooking Zuñi Wash. Two were across the highway, where a newer portion of the village clustered around the Catholic school. Not only was the crowd **thus fragmented, but it ebbed and flowed** between these houses. Leaphorn had moved with it, watching the dark streets, checking the clusters of people around vehicles, pushing through the **jam-packed** viewing galleries and through the **throngs** eating lamb stew, canned peaches, and bakery cookies in the Zuñi kitchens, always looking for the face he had memorized from the Zuñi school yearbook.

....

thus fragmented, but it ebbed and flowed split apart, but
they came and went
jam-packed crowded
throngs groups of people

Once he had seen Pasquaanti, who seemed to have some ceremonial role at the Shalako house near Saint Anthony's school. Leaphorn had caught the Zuñi's attention, called him out into the darkness, and told him quickly and briefly his conclusions about who had killed Ernesto Cata. Pasquaanti had listened silently, commenting only with a nod. Later Leaphorn had noticed Baker, huddled in a bulky fur-collared coat, leaning against a post on the porch of the house where the Council of the Gods was dancing. Baker glanced at Leaphorn—a glance totally without recognition—and then had looked away. He obviously did not want to be seen talking to a man in the uniform of the Navajo Police. Leaphorn stood for a few moments well down the porch, curious. Beyond the porch, the yard was crowded with an assortment of vehicles. Baker looked either drunk or sleepy, perhaps both. He was watching a young man who stood in the back door of a camper talking to a young woman in a heavy mackinaw. Leaphorn felt a sudden impulse to walk up to Baker, grab him by the **lapels**, and tell him about Bowlegs, asking him to forget about this manhunt for an hour and help find the Navajo boy. Baker would be good at it, smart, fast, always thinking. **But the impulse died aborning.** Baker would simply smile that silly smile and refuse to be distracted from whomever he was stalking. Leaphorn thought he would not like to be hunted by Baker.

At 1 A.M., when Leaphorn decided he wouldn't find Bowlegs, he was in the left gallery room of one of the Shalako houses on the hill. The bruise on his stomach ached with a

....

lapels front of his jacket

But the impulse died aborning. But the feeling ended quickly.

steady throb. His eyes burned with tobacco smoke, incense, and stale air. He had finally worked his way up to the long window that looked down into the spectators jamming the benches and chairs in the dirt-floored room below him. He had scanned carefully every face visible through the opposite gallery. Now he leaned heavily on the sill and let mind and muscles relax. He was very tired. Almost directly below him and to his left, a wooden altar stood, its base bristling with rows of feathered prayer plumes. Next to it the drummers and flutists produced an **intricate counterpointed rhythm** which never seemed to repeat its complicated pattern. And on the floor, sunken four feet or more below ground level solely to permit this, the giant Shalako danced.

From where Leaphorn stood by the gallery window on the floor above, he was almost at eye level with the great bird. Its beak snapped suddenly—a half-dozen sharp clacking sounds in perfect time with the drum. It hooted and its strange white-rimmed eyes stared for a moment directly into Leaphorn's. The policeman saw it with double vision. He saw it as a mask **of tremendous technical ingenuity**, a device of leather, embroidered cotton, carved wood, feathers, and paint held aloft on a pole, its beak and its movements manipulated by the dancer within it. But he also saw Shalako, the **courier** between the gods and men, who brought fertility to the seeds and rain to the desert when the people of Zuñi called, and who came on this great day to be fed and blessed by his people. Now it danced, swooping down the earthen floor, its great

....

intricate counterpointed rhythm complicated contrasting rhythm

of tremendous technical ingenuity that was very hard to make

courier messenger

horns glittering with reflected light, its fan of topknot feathers bristling, its voice the hooting call of the night birds.

There was a sudden shift in the cadence of the music. The voices of the chanters rose in pitch. The Koyemshi had joined the Shalako on the floor. Mudheads, they were called. Their bodies were coated with a pinkish clay and their masks gave them heads distorted in shape, hairless, knobbed, with tiny rimmed eyes and puckered mouths. They represented the idiotic and **deformed** fruits of incest—that ultimate tribal taboo. The first Koyemshi, as Leaphorn remembered the mythology, were the offspring of a son and daughter of Shiwanni, the Sun Father. He had sent his children to help the Zuñi in their search for the Middle Place, but the boy had had intercourse with his sister. And the same night ten children were born. The first was normal and was to be the ancestor of the makers of rain. But the next nine were deformed and insane. Leaphorn considered this, his head buzzing with fatigue. The Mudheads represented evil and yet they were perhaps the most **prestigious** fraternity of this people. The men who represented the ten **offspring** were chosen to play this role for a year. They helped build the ceremonial houses and were involved in a year-long series of retreats, fastings, and ritual dancing. The assignment was so demanding of time that it wasn't unusual for a Mudhead to have to quit his job for a year and depend on the support of the villagers.

Leaphorn watched them dance. Despite the snow falling outside, they were nude except for black breechcloth and neck

....

deformed oddly shaped
prestigious honored, respected
offspring children

scarf, moccasins and mask. Their dance was intricate, a fast and exact placement of foot, their deerskin seed pouches slapping against sweat-damp ribs, their hands shaking feathered wands, their voices rising now in yells of triumph, and falling into the rhythmic recitation of the **saga** of their people.

Leaphorn scanned the crowd again. Below him there were mostly women—Zuñis in their ceremonial best, a scattering of Navajos, a blond girl, her face ashen with fatigue but her eyes bright with interest. To his right, two young Navajo men had edged their way near the window. They were discussing a young white man, who wore his hair in braids, had a red headband around his forehead and a heavy silver concho belt.

"I think he's **an albino Indian**," one said. "Ask him if he can say something in Navajo." The voice was loud enough for the white man to hear. "I think he's an Apache," the other Navajo said. "He looks too much like an Indian to be a Navajo."

They were drinking, Leaphorn saw. Not quite drunk, but drunk enough to **slip over the boundary between humor and rudeness**. If he weren't so tired, and otherwise occupied, he would move them out into the cold sobering air. Instead he would himself move from here, where George Bowlegs obviously wasn't, back to the Longhorn House for another check there. As he decided this, he saw George Bowlegs.

The boy was across the dance room, in the opposite gallery. He seemed to be standing on something, perhaps a chair, looking over the heads of those pressed against the windowsill—staring almost directly toward Leaphorn at the

....

saga long story

an albino Indian a Native American without any color

slip over the boundary between humor and rudeness act rudely

Shalako swooping down the dance floor. Leaphorn recognized him instantly. The generous mouth, the large expressive eyes, and the short-cropped hair. More than that. Even in that crowded gallery there was something about the boy that suggested the strange and the lonely. George stared at the dancing gods with eyes that were fixed and fascinated and a little crazy. He was no farther away than the width of the dance room. Perhaps a dozen yards.

Leaphorn began pushing his way back from the window, struggling through the **packed humanity** toward the passageway that ran behind the dance room to connect the two galleries. He moved as fast as he could, leaving a wake of jostled spectators, bruised feet, and curses. The passageway, too, was blocked with watchers. It took him two full minutes to fight his way through to the doorway. It was blocked as well. Finally he was in the right gallery. A Navajo woman was standing on the chair Bowlegs had used. He pushed his way through the crowd, looking frantically. The boy was nowhere.

Outside, Leaphorn thought. He must have gone out.

Outside the snow was falling heavily. Leaphorn pulled up his collar, gave his eyes a second to adjust, and peered into the darkness. A party of **Anglos**, loud and drunk, came around the corner toward the door where Leaphorn stood. And something—no more than a glimpse of movement—disappeared in the alleyway between the Shalako house and another of the cut stone houses of old Zuñi. Leaphorn followed **at a trot**. The alley was cut off from all light—utterly dark.

----

packed humanity crowds
Anglos white people
at a trot quickly

Leaphorn ran down it and stopped at its **mouth**.

The alley opened into the unlit plaza just above the mission church. A small figure was now moving across it at a slow walk. Leaphorn stopped, peered through the sifting snow. Was it George? At that moment began a series of events which Leaphorn never quite straightened out in his memory. First, from the blackness of another alleyway, there came a wavering, hooting call. The walking figure stopped, turned, shouted something joyful which might have been the Navajo word for "yes!" And Leaphorn stood for some small **measure** of time, undecided. Whatever time he wasted—two ticks of his watch, or five—became time enough for George Bowlegs to die.

Leaphorn moved just as the boy's figure disappeared into the mouth of darkness. He moved frantically. His boots skidded on the wet snow and he fell heavily on his hands. And when he had scrambled again to his feet, he had lost another two or three seconds. It was then that he heard the sound. Actually, a double sound. Thump-crack. Loud but muffled. He pulled his pistol from his holster as he ran. At the alley opening he stopped, knowing he was too late. He was. George Bowlegs lay on his side just inside the alley. Leaphorn crouched beside him. And then there was another sound. This one a thump, followed by a muffled yell, followed by a **scuffling**, followed by silence. Leaphorn moved cautiously down the alley, hearing nothing now, seeing nothing. He pulled his flashlight from his coat pocket. The heavy snow ahead of him bore a single set of boot prints and then, at the empty doorway of an abandoned

....

mouth opening, entrance
measure amount
scuffling struggle

home, a jumble of footprints, and on the snow a plume of feathers. Leaphorn thought he recognized the plume. It was the decoration that had topped the fierce mask of the Salamobia.

Leaphorn flashed his light down the alley. The boot prints stopped here. Whoever had made them must have gone, or been taken, into the empty building. Leaphorn flashed his light through the doorway. There was fresh snow on the **earthen floor**. Part of it had sifted in through the broken roof and part had come from the feet of men. He flashed the light around, saw nothing, and ran back up the alley to where George Bowlegs lay. He knelt in the snow, his face against the boy's, hoping to feel a breath. The sacred wind of your life I breathe, Leaphorn thought. But the sacred wind was gone.

Snowflakes sifted through the beam of the flashlight, dusting the boy's tangled hair with white, clinging to an eyelash, melting on the still-warm face. Leaphorn gently turned the body and felt through the pockets of the ragged jacket. In the side pocket he found a case knife, a dime, some piñon nuts, a stub of pencil, a folding magnifying glass, the tiny figure of a bear carved from turquoise. He had seen the magnifying glass before, among the odds and ends in the ransacked hogan of Shorty Bowlegs. George must have stopped at the hogan on his way here from the mesa and found it abandoned. He would have seen the hole knocked in its wall, recognized the mark of the death hogan, and known that now he was even more alone than he had been.

It was then that Leaphorn noticed the prayer plume. George

....

earthen floor ground

must have been carrying it in his hand, holding it out, offering it. And when **the bullet struck**, the boy had fallen on it. It was beautifully made, its willow butt smoothed and painted, its blue-and-yellow songbird feathers neatly arranged. And tied to the willow with a thong was the cold stone symmetry of a perfect Stone Age lance point. This one unbroken—slender, formed with parallel flaking, a relic from seven or eight thousand years in the past—a perfect offering to the gods.

Leaphorn took off his jacket and spread it carefully over the face of George Bowlegs. From somewhere in the dark across the plaza he heard the brief sound of flutes and chanting as a door opened and closed at one of the Shalako houses. Behind him there was the mutter of conversation. Three people, huddled in their coats against the snow, hurried across the plaza and disappeared in the alley toward the Shalako house he had left. No one seemed to have heard the muffled shot. No one except whoever had seized the killer and pulled him into the empty house. Leaphorn walked back down the alley, keeping against the wall and examining the footprints in the snow. The killer had been running. He wore boots. Size ten, Leaphorn guessed. Perhaps eleven. Apparently he had seen Leaphorn after he had fired the shot. But as he passed this doorway someone, something, had stopped him. Leaphorn studied the trampled snow, but already the tracks were softened and blurred by fresh-falling flakes.

Inside the empty building, Leaphorn took his time. There was no longer any reason to hurry and he **meticulously** sorted

....

the bullet struck he got shot
meticulously carefully

out what the snow tracks had to tell him. There had been three persons wearing moccasins. Leading from the alley into the doorway there were drag marks left by boot heels. The moccasins trailed snow through two empty rooms, left fresh tracks in a third, roofless room, and then departed over a fallen wall onto the street. Here the tracks indicated that two of the men **bore a heavy burden**. Leaphorn followed them for perhaps fifty yards. The tracks were fading fast and he lost them where they crossed a village street that had been heavily used. He was motivated only by a mild curiosity now. Everything was finished.

Back in the alley, he stared down at the body of George Bowlegs. Snow had whitened Leaphorn's coat and the boy's too-small denims. Leaphorn squatted and picked up the dead boy, his arms under the legs and shoulders. He guessed he was again violating O'Malley's procedures by moving the body. But he would not allow this boy to lie here alone in the icy darkness. He walked out of the alley, **cradling** the body, surprised at how light it seemed. And then stopped, **conscious of a final irony**. He was taking Bowlegs home. But where was home for this boy who had hunted heaven?

....

bore a heavy burden carried something heavy

cradling holding

conscious of a final irony realizing something interesting but sad

⪢ **20** ⪡

Sunday, December 7, 9 A.M.

Inside Ted Isaacs' homemade camper, it was an odd mixture of hot and cold. Outside, the landscape was a white wilderness of blowing snow, and the camper groaned and creaked with the buffeting gusts. The kerosene heater roared, but icy air seeped through cracks and crevices, eddying around Leaphorn's snow-covered boots and up the legs of his trousers.

"I can't say I expected any company today," Isaacs said, "but I'm glad you came. **When this lets up** and they get the roads opened a little, I'm going to that commune and see about Susie. And I wanted to ask—"

"She left yesterday," Leaphorn said. "Halsey kicked her out. She went with me hunting for George Bowlegs Thursday and the last time I saw her she was at the Zuñi police station. That was about noon yesterday. The federal officers were talking to her."

"Where is she now?" Isaacs said. "Is she still there?"

"I don't know," Leaphorn said.

"My God!" Isaacs said. "I hope she isn't out in this snow." He looked at Leaphorn. "She didn't have anyplace to go."

....

When this lets up When it stops snowing

"Yeah," Leaphorn said. "That's what I was telling you a couple of days ago." He didn't try to keep the anger from his voice. "Here, I came to bring you something." He fished the broken lance tip from his pocket and handed it to Isaacs.

"Parallel flaked," Isaacs said. "Where'd you fi . . ." His voice trailed off. He turned abruptly to the file case, jerked open a drawer, and **rummaged**. When he closed the drawer he had a second piece of flint in his hand.

"George Bowlegs had it," Leaphorn said. "He buried it where he killed a deer over southwest of here. Sort of a fetish offering."

Isaacs was staring at him.

"Does it match?" Leaphorn asked. "It does, doesn't it?"

"I think so." The anthropologist put both pieces on the Formica table, the broken butt he had slipped out of the envelope from the filing cabinet and the tip Bowlegs had buried. Both were of pinkish streaked **silicified wood**. Isaacs' fingers adjusted them. They fit perfectly.

Isaacs looked up, his face strained. "Man," he said. "If Reynolds finds out that boy got this, he'll kill me." He paused. "But how could he have gotten it? I never let him do any digging out there. Or any sorting, either. He couldn't have . . ."

"Cata gave it to him," Leaphorn said. "Cata stole it out of that box in the back of Reynolds' pickup truck, along with some other artifacts. Like I told you the last time I was out here. And he gave some of it to George."

"But Reynolds said nothing was missing," Isaacs said. He

....

rummaged searched inside it
silicified wood wood made hard like a rock

paused, staring at Leaphorn. "Wait a minute," he said. "He couldn't have gotten this out of Reynolds' truck. Reynolds couldn't have had it." He stopped again. Suddenly he looked sick.

"He couldn't have, but he did," Leaphorn said. "Reynolds was **salting** the site. Isn't that your word for it? Salting? Anyway, he was **planting stuff** for you to find."

"I don't believe it," Isaacs said. He sat down. His stricken face said he did believe it. His eyes were looking past Leaphorn at the wreckage of everything.

"Ernesto did his little bit of stealing just at the wrong time," Leaphorn said. "It spoiled a lot of work. Reynolds had gotten himself a supply of the sort of flint Folsom Man liked. That was easy enough. And then he prepared his evidence. I'd guess he made some bits and pieces of paralleled-flaked artifacts. He'd have saved the chips and the broken stuff and all. And then he started roughing out some pressure-flaked Folsom-type artifacts from the very same patterned flint. He didn't really need the fine finished product—which you say is hard to counterfeit. All he needed was the unfinished, broken stuff." Leaphorn paused, waiting for Isaacs to say something. Isaacs stared blindly at the wall. "Maybe the Reynolds theory is true," Leaphorn said. "It sounds sensible enough. But I guess Reynolds wasn't willing to wait to prove it. That ridicule must have **infuriated him**. He wanted to make his critics **eat crow**."

"Yeah," Isaacs said.

"I don't exactly know how he did it. Probably made himself

---

salting secretly placing fake artifacts in
planting stuff secretly placing things
infuriated him made him really angry
eat crow admit they were wrong

214

some sort of tonglike gadget to hold the flint and punch them down to the hard layer where you were finding the stuff. He couldn't do it in advance because he had to place the planted stuff in the right location relative to the genuine artifacts you were finding."

"Yeah," Isaacs said. "He'd check in here a lot about sundown or so and we'd go over what I'd found and where I'd find it. And then while I was cooking supper, he'd take his flashlight and go out there and inspect the dig. That would be when he did it. And that's why everything seemed to fit so perfectly." Isaacs slammed his fist into his palm. "My God! It was perfect. Nobody could have even argued." He looked up at Leaphorn. "And then Cata stole some of the stuff he was planting. So Reynolds killed Cata?"

"Do you think that's enough reason for him to kill the boy?" Leaphorn asked. It was something that puzzled him.

"Of course," Isaacs said. "Hell, yes. Once he found out some of his artifacts were missing and Cata had 'em, I guess he'd have to do it." Leaphorn's doubt seemed to puzzle Isaacs. "Maybe you don't know how serious it would be to salt a site. My God! It's unthinkable. This whole science is based on everybody being **beyond suspicion**. When **this gets out** Reynolds will be worse than finished. Nobody will touch him, or his books, or trust anything he ever had anything to do with." Isaacs slumped on his stool, contemplating. "It's like—" he began. But he could think of **no suitably hideous analogy**.

Like murdering a boy, Leaphorn thought. Worse than that,

....

beyond suspicion trustworthy

this gets out people hear about this

no suitably hideous analogy nothing bad enough to compare it to

obviously, in Isaacs' view. Even worse than three murders. In Isaacs' scale of values, killing was a simple byproduct of the serious offense, something Reynolds would need to do to protect his reputation.

"It's just unthinkable," Isaacs concluded. "How did you figure it out?"

"Remember when you found the parts of those broken points right together? That bothered me. It would seem more natural when you've spent an hour trying to make something and all of a sudden it breaks to **lose your temper** and throw it half a mile. You don't just politely drop it at your feet. Not if it keeps happening."

"I guess that bothered me a little, too," Isaacs said. "Only I didn't let myself think about it."

"When Reynolds chased Cata away from the truck he must have checked right away and found some of his stuff was gone." Leaphorn fished the unbroken point from his pocket and handed it to Isaacs. "This had been taken, too, and probably other material. It was bad enough Cata having it. But *when* he **got it was fatal**. What if he got a guilty conscience and brought it back and gave it to you? You'd ask where he got it and when, and then you'd have known Reynolds was putting the stuff in the ground for you to find. Or if the site got to be famous— and Reynolds knew that would happen—then Cata was sure to talk."

"So he went out to kill Cata," Isaacs said. "Well, that makes sense."

....

lose your temper become angry
got it was fatal chose to steal it caused him to get killed

216

"I think he just went out to get the stuff back. I think he rigged himself up a kachina mask so Cata wouldn't recognize him and planned to scare the boy into giving him the stuff. But the boy tried to get away from him."

"If you haven't arrested him yet, he's supposed to be in Tucson this weekend, but he's coming back Monday," Isaacs said.

"He wasn't in Tucson. When Reynolds killed Cata he found the boy had just part of the missing stuff with him. The most damaging pieces were missing. And then he learned that Bowlegs had been here with him. So Bowlegs must have this most important **fragment**." Leaphorn tapped the broken lance tip. "You'd already found the butt and Bowlegs had the tip. So he had to go hunting for George. He had to catch him and make sure he got the tip back before he could kill him. Now Reynolds was covering up a murder, too. He wore the kachina mask when he was prowling around the commune seeing if George was there. If someone saw Reynolds, Reynolds was in trouble. If somebody reported seeing a kachina, you'd think they were crazy, or drunk, or just **superstitious**."

"But he didn't get George, did he?" Isaacs said suddenly. "He didn't get George?"

"He killed George last night," Leaphorn said. "He almost caught him Friday night, and when George came back to Zuñi, where we could pick him up, he simply had to kill him. I guess he figured that even if we found the artifact we'd have a hell of a time proving anything without George to **testify**."

....

fragment piece
superstitious believed in things that were not real
testify tell what happened in court

"You'll need this, then." Isaacs pushed the broken point toward him. "That'll be some evidence, anyway. I'll bet you can **hang him**."

"We'll never find him," Leaphorn said. "I guess you'd say there's an old law that **takes precedence over the white man's penal code**. It says 'Thou shall not **profane** the Sacred Ways of Zuñi.'" He explained to Isaacs about the footprints in the alley. "I don't think anybody is ever going to know what happened to Reynolds. A few days from now, somebody will come across his pickup wherever he left it and he'll go into the records as a missing person."

He pushed the point back toward Isaacs.

"I don't need these," Leaphorn said. "The FBI has jurisdiction in this business and the FBI isn't interested in Indian superstitions and broken stones and all that. It's got another solution in mind."

Isaacs picked up the points, juggled them in his palm. Then he stared at Leaphorn.

"Do whatever you want to do," Leaphorn said. "I'm finished with all of this. I had just one little job. I screwed it up. I was supposed to find George Bowlegs. He's found, but not soon enough. I told the FBI man what I saw and what I heard last night. But I didn't tell him what I guessed. He didn't ask me, and I didn't tell him."

"What you're saying is that nobody but you and I and Reynolds knows this site was **fixed**," Isaacs said. "And you're saying Reynolds is dead . . ."

....

hang him prove that he is guilty
takes precedence over the white man's penal code is more important than the white man's law
profane abuse
fixed fake

"And I'm saying that when I leave here, I'm going to the Ramah chapter house and get back to work on a deal involving a down payment on a pickup truck."

Isaacs was still staring at him, wordlessly.

"Come on," Leaphorn said. "Can't you understand what I'm saying?" His voice was angry. He took the lance tip from Isaacs' palm, opened the jaws of the vise on the workbench, and held the flint between them while he screwed the vise closed. Under the pressure, the flint crumbled into fragments. "I'm saying," Leaphorn gritted through his teeth, "just how much do you want fame and fortune and a faculty job? A couple of days ago you wanted it worse than you wanted that girl of yours. How about now? You want it bad enough to lie a little? I'm saying nobody's going to guess this bastard of a dig was salted unless you tell them it was—and then maybe they won't believe you. Who in hell would believe the great Chester Reynolds would salt a dig? You think they'd believe a Navajo cop?" Leaphorn dusted the flint dust from his fingers. "A cop who doesn't have **a shred of evidence**?"

Joe Leaphorn opened the camper door and stepped out in the snow. "I'm trying to learn more about white men," he said. "You wanted all that worse than you wanted your woman. What else will you give up for it?"

He'd left his carryall on the shoulder of the highway. The motor was still warm and it started easily, the chains making a **muted** song where the wind had left clear spots on the pavement. He would make a circle up N.M. 53 to Interstate

....

a shred of evidence any proof
muted quiet

40 in case Susie was trying to hitchhike, and if she was he'd give her a ride into Gallup and loan her the ten-dollar bill he had in his **billfold**. And maybe someday he would write a note to O'Malley and let him know who killed Ernesto Cata. But probably not.

....

billfold wallet

BEFORE YOU MOVE ON...

1. **Summarize** Reread pages 214–215. Why did the killer murder Ernesto Cata and George Bowlegs?

2. **Theme** How does the plot of the story relate to the theme Twists and Turns?